The Prince Presents, LLC

The Tommy Good Story III
"Life After Death"

The Final Chapter!

www.theprincepresents.com
www.streetknowledgepublishing.com

NOTE:

Publisher: The Prince Presents, LLC
P.O. Box 25042 Wilmington, DE 19899
www.theprincepresents.com

ISBN# 13: 978-1508655312

The Tommy Good Story III Credits
Story by: Leondrei Prince
Typed and Edited by: Turmesha "Mesha" Sturgis
Typeset Layout: Linda Williams
Cover Graphics by: "L.R." at followthefuture@aol.com

Special Thanks to: Black and Nobel Book Store

Printed in Canada

Acknowledgments

First of all there is no other being on deity worthy of praise except Allah…There would be no me without him. All my thanks go out to Him…Allah Akbar!!

I'm back again y'all….

Table Of Contents

Table Of Contents

Chapter One

Mike folded his cell phone closed then looked around the church good before putting it back in his pocket. Never once did he lose faith or underestimate the power of Aunt Ertha's mojo. He just didn't know how long it would take. "Not long at all," he smiled to himself at the thought of Tommy's voice and laughter just seconds ago on his phone. Today marked a new day. The day of life after death for the man known as Tommy Good, and Mike's mood couldn't have been greater than it was now. He had his brother from another mother back and couldn't wait to get down Louisiana to see him.

Robin sat next to her sister Raven, blown by what she had just told her. She couldn't believe she allowed herself to become pregnant by this dead man, but she had. Then she thought, "Well the baby is innocent. It's not its fault. Let's just pray it's healthy, Al-Hum-Du-Allah," Robin continued to think as she couldn't help but notice Mike on his cell phone. "Damn—that's odd. Who would he be talking to at Tommy's funeral?" she questioned and couldn't come up with anything logical. So she just kept her focus on him. When he smiled after folding his phone up, the eeriest feeling Robin ever felt in her life slowly eased up her backbone, and she felt Satan's (the Devil's) presence. For some odd reason Robin knew Tommy Good was alive, especially now since she looked at the head of the church and there was no body. Instantly a fear she never knew overcame her, and she began to shake violently until she passed out.

"Somebody help!" she heard Raven yell, but she couldn't move. All she could do was replay the scenes of that night she pretended to be Raven and tried to take Tommy's life. "He didn't die then, so what means he's dead now?" was all she could think of. Then Tommy's laughter erupted in her head. "Nooooo!" she screamed then sat straight up drenched in her own sweat.

"Are you ok?" someone asked.

"Yes, I'm fine. I'm sorry, but I have to go," Robin said and ran out the church.

That was seven months ago to today and Robin sometimes felt Tommy's presence, sometimes stronger than others. Like today as she stood on the side of her sister's hospital bed holding her hand while the doctor yelled, "Push Raven! I can see the baby's head," Raven bit down on her bottom lip, closed her eyes, and then pushed with everything she had left in her until she felt a rip from her slit to her ass and the life of her child slip from between her legs. "It's a Boy!"

"What are you going to name him?" one of the nurses who assisted asked.

"Tommy Good Jr.," Raven said proudly.

■ ■ ■ ■ ■

Becoming a new mother for the first time was an experience you only experienced once because every time after that you know what to expect. That's what made the first time so special. It was a whole new introduction into womanhood and life. It was a time when the first-time mother experienced body changes, sicknesses, and emotions she couldn't control. There was days when Raven would be so happy she would cry. Then there were days when she'd be so scared and sad that she would cry. But all in all she'd make it out of any emotional roller coaster smiling with her head held high, like now as she tucked her son in and thought back on all the shit her family and friends, along with some of her college professors told her.

"Raven, think about what you're doing."

"Are you sure you want to have this baby?"

"What about your future? Finish college first, you can always have another baby," they would say, and she would think, "Yeah, but not by Tommy."

"Get an abortion," some even said, but there was no way in the world she was killing her baby. "Yeah right," she said aloud and sarcastic at the memory of that last statement, then pulled the blanket up on Tommy Jr. Looking down at the spitting image of the man she once loved, she knew that an abortion would have been the worst mistake of her life. Damn how she missed Tommy. Raven walked away from the baby's bassinette that was only feet away from her bed, then flopped down on it. She kicked her huge oversized pink bunny slippers off, then pulled her feet up into Indian style, and reached for her book on the nightstand. The book was called: "Sincerely Yours" by Al Sadiq Banks, and she could not put it down. It was almost like that with all the urban books she read, especially the ones by Al Sadiq, J.M. Benjamin, Kwan, Treasure Blue, T. Styles, and Wahida Clark. But her favorite of them all was a local named Leondrei Prince, some dude from Riverside by way of New Castle, "Cash Ave." to be exact. In fact, that was the name of his latest novel, a story in which he held nothing back by sharing a part of his life, his addiction, and his love for the women of the night that took care of him like family for three whole years. To Raven it was a book that set him apart from all the rest because he let you know who he really was as a person. You no longer had to guess about what your author was really like; he gave it to you from the horse's mouth. "Big ups Lee Mudd," Raven thought, and then dived back into her book.

Falling back into the groove of her pages, time was elapsing faster and faster. She looked over at her digital clock/radio by Bose and noticed it was nearly 10 p.m. "Damn! Let me put this book down knowing I got school tomorrow," she said thinking of this being her last semester of the school year. This year and next year was all Raven had left before she earned her degree in medicine from Temple University, and she knew then she'd be raking in some real good money as if she needed it anyway. Because since the day Tommy died, Mike and Ann had been there for Raven like nothing she could have imagined or even fixed herself to ask for. She didn't have a want in the world. Mike even brought her a new BMW 5 Series to carry her back and forth to Temple from the house out Pike Creek that Marcus, Tommy's brother, had given her. It was the same house Tommy had built for Big Mom that she refused to take. So money wasn't really an issue for Raven because she gave birth to the "Good" family. However, being independent was something she always was. Raven was not into handouts or IOUs.

After Raven had gotten everything in order for her and her son for tomorrow, she got back in the bed. She didn't have to worry about daycare because Ann, Mike's wife was not having that. "Oh, hell no!" she told Raven when Raven asked about a good daycare. "My nephew is not going to any daycare yet! Girl, he is too young. Now we might let him go once he starts talking, but as for now he ain't going nowhere but here with me and the kids."

"Ann what would I do without you?" Raven said that day, and Ann has been there faithfully every since. Every morning like clockwork, Ann is at the door waiting to take Tommy Jr. With that, Raven rolled over on her side and tried to get some sleep. Then her phone rang.

"Hello," she answered, and no one responded. "Hello!" she said again. "Look, I'm a grown ass woman, and I have shit to do in the morning like college and tending to my son. It is too late at night for you to be playing on my phone. So I'm asking you like a woman, can you please find someone else's phone to play on? Thanks," she said and hung up. The crank calls had been coming regularly now over the past week and Raven was thinking, "That's it! I'm changing my damn number."

Chapter Two

New Orleans, Louisiana, the boot shaped state known for being the home and birthplace to jazz, the Lindy-Hop dance, and the "The Mardi Gras" had a new sheriff in town, and his name was "Reno", a name giving to him by his new team of assembled "Goons" he especially hand-picked himself. They gave him the name "Reno" because it was rumored that his money was just as long, if not longer than the casinos in Reno, Nevada, a heavy statement for a young black man who just popped up in the 9th Ward section. The section most heavily damaged by "Katrina" nearly a year ago. So now, as he cruised Bourbon St. in his new Rolls Royce Phantom headed to his favorite Jazz joint to ease some tension at the hands, lips, and fingertips of this bad ass redbone broad he know as "Lady" who played the saxophone, he enjoyed the ever so familiar smell that filled his car through his cracked windows and open sunroof. The smell that was just as familiar to your nose as the sight of a major league baseball player with a jaw full of sunflower seeds was to your eyes. The smell of "Gumbo" and crawfish, mixed in with the swampy smell of the Mississippi river blowing in from the shore. Reno loved his new home, but nothing compared to "Home-Home", and more times than none he missed the "Small Wonder, The First State".

Dressed in a tailor-made suit by Pierre Hardy worth nearly $7,000.00 with a shoe to match, also by Pierre Hardy that cost him a cool $3,000.00, Reno stepped out of his Phantom at the Jazz joint called: "Kansas City's" and headed in.

"Good evening Mr. Reno," the Maitre d' said. "Your table is ready this way, sir."

"Thanks, uh?"

"Scott."

"Yeah, Scott," Reno said and followed him to his table right in front of the stage where "Lady" was leading the house band with the sax as they played an old George Howard joint. She smiled when she saw Reno seated, and he acknowledged the gesture with a wink of his eye.

To women, Reno was what you called a ladies' man. Standing at a cool 6'2" with an athletic build, he could easily have been mistaken for a model. You know the new wave rugged looking model. Reno had a torso and both his arms sleeved with tattoos. Dark eerie tattoos, like skulls, witches, crystal balls, grave yards, and shit like that, but they still looked good. His newly twisted dreadlocks hung shoulder length, and his face was full of tattoo tears, and when he smiled or talked you couldn't help but notice his diamond and platinum grill. His mouth looked like a seventies disco ball that hung over a dance floor.

"Hi sir, my name is Patricia, but people call me Pat. Is there anything I can help you with?" the hour glass shaped waitress asked him then held her hand out to be shaken as a formal introduction.

"Hey Pat, my name is Tommy, Tommy Good, but my folks call me Reno," he stated in his newly found heavy southern accent, and held out his manicured hand to shake hers back.

"Nice to meet you," she said nearly mesmerized by this man's presence, as she shook his hand. And just as natural as it was to breathe, her eyes did a complete once over of the man before her. His look and style of dress gave off the perfect gentleman/businessman persona, as did his expensive cologne. However, the way his knuckle was pushed back into his hand probably from a punch he threw somewhere in his past, gave her the notion there was a darker side to this man whose nails were freshly manicured.

"Uh, are you going to let go and allow me to order?" Tommy asked.

"Oh my God! I am so sorry. Please forgive me sir. Uh, what is it that you'll be having?" Pat asked trying to shake away the embarrassment of being caught totally lusting by the man she was lusting over.

"It's ok Hun. I'll have a dirty, extra dirty martini and Modella's beer please."

"Ok. Coming right up," she said and raced off.

"Oh!" Tommy called before she got out of ear's reach, "and a plate of crawfish and gumbo," he called out and she nodded with approval. Tommy mumbled, "Mmm-Mmm-Mmm," under his breath as she switched away. Pat's ass looked as soft as a bag of water that held a brand new goldfish from a pet store. And to give him an eyeful because she knew he was watching, she put more of a bounce into the jiggle and looked over her shoulder with a smile. Tommy was so caught up in the moment that he never noticed the band had stopped playing until he felt the playful slap upside his head.

"Damn Reno! What color are her thongs or is she wearing any?" Lady said with a slight hint of jealousy in her voice.

"Oh shit! My bad. Was I that obvious?"

"Is it Red Snapper in the Colorado river, nigga?" she asked him and they shared a laugh.

"Here have a seat," Tommy told her and pulled out an empty chair that was at his table. "So what's up? Y'all done for tonight or do y'all got another set to play?

"Nah, we done for tonight, they got this new band about to play a few sets of "Groover" and I he'ah they like that too. Fo'sho," Lady talked in the heavy New 'Awlins accent she had since a child. "I'm only fit'na stay for maybe two songs cause a bitch tired and winded," she said. "I've been blowin' that sax since happy hour." And soon as the words rolled off her tongue she knew she set herself up.

Tommy couldn't help himself; he had to get her so he looked down at his watch and said, "Since happy hour? Damn that's like four hours! Why I can't ever get blown like that?" he said with a laugh.

"Cause you can only stand for two minutes," she shot back on cue, turning Tommy's laugh into a frown. Before he could respond, the waitress, Pat was bringing back his order.

"Here's your order Reno," she said and shot Lady a look.

"Thank you Pat," Tommy said letting her know he remembered her name.

"Will there be anything else?" Pat asked and to return the gesture of Pat's cold stare, Lady said, "No, that will be all thank you," and picked through Tommy's crawfish. "We'll holla at you when we need the bill." "Stank bitch," Pat thought and responded back with a, "Will you be able to pay the bill being as though you play for a band on the chitterling circuit?" and walked off leaving her to ponder on those words. Tommy smirked.

"Baby did you hear that shit?" Lady asked Tommy.

"Yeah I heard her baby. What you expected her to say beings though you're with something she's attracted to?" Tommy asked her.

"Boy you are too conceited for me," Lady said. "Now come on, I'm riding home with you tonight."

"Where's your car?"

"I didn't drive it. I knew you would be here tonight."

"How you know that?"

"How could I not know?" Look at me," she said. "Now let me go in the back and grab my instruments."

As soon as Lady disappeared behind the backstage, Tommy called Pat over paying the bill, leaving a healthy tip, and jotting his number down on a napkin.

"Tell the lady I was with that I'm out in my car. And be nice, for me," he said, and stood to leave. Being around both those women had him missing Raven so he needed some time alone in his car before Lady came outside to it. He pulled out his cell phone, blocked the number and called Raven like he'd been doing over the past month.

"Hello," Raven answered. "Hello! Look, I'm a grown ass woman and I have shit to do!" she rambled on before hanging up.

"Damn I miss my baby," Tommy thought. He was the crank caller.

■■■■■■

When Lady came out of "Kansas City's" Jazz Club in the heart of historical New Orleans Bourbon St. carrying her two instruments, a sax and a horn, Tommy got out to help her load them in his trunk. "Thanks baby," she said to Tommy, but when he didn't answer her, she looked at him closely before shutting the trunk, noticing his sudden mood swing, and didn't say anything else. She figured it would be better for him to break the ice with conversation instead of her because she didn't know what mood he was in. This was something that Lady had gotten used to over the past six months of them dating. She had come to the conclusion that Tommy was bipolar and left it at that. As to the reasons why? and how?, he could go from "hot" to "cold" in the blink of an eye like that was still a mystery to her. What she did know was that eyes were the key to the soul, and Tommy's told her a tale of a man with a troubled past.

Tommy noticed Lady still staring at him like she was outside the car and realized that his silence was unfair to her. It wasn't her fault that he was all the way down here in New Orleans hiding out from a past that could mean a lengthy prison sentence. Faking your death was indeed a crime, but did he actually fake his death? The coroner pronounced him dead on the scene on Bennett St. that night, so was he faking his death? It was something that he wasn't trying to find out willingly though. His plan was to lay low for seven years until the statute of limitations on the alleged crime ran out before going home, however plans didn't always go as planned. They sometimes fell through. Tommy looked over to Lady and placed his hand on her thick thigh when he jumped on I-

10 and headed west to his new home on the outer limits of the N.O.

"Baby I'm sorry about my silence, ok. It's just that sometimes my mind goes blank and a nigga gets lost in his own thoughts, you dig?

"Boy I don't pay you no mind when you do that shit. I diagnosed you a long time ago as bipolar," she laughed, causing Tommy to laugh too.

"Oh, so I'm crazy, huh?"

"Are you?" Lady asked as they pulled on to the freshly paved dirt driveway that led up to the old slave plantation ran by the Jefferson's that Tommy just had to buy. There was no way he was going to let some cracker buy it back and reminisce with generations to come about how black women were raped on this land, and black men were hung from these same trees. He was putting an end to that shit once and for all. Tommy parked in front of the huge mansion that mirrored the huge house on the hill in the movie, "Gone With The Wind" and led Lady to the front door. No sooner than he could find his key to the house did the front door swing open and standing there was his butler Mr. Jefferson, a third generation slave owner that now worked for Tommy in the same house he grew up in as a child. The thought alone made Tommy smile. "What's up Bentley?" he teased.

"Nothing Mr. Good. How was your evening?"

"Better than yours," Tommy said and brushed by the old white man. Mr. Jefferson turned beet red and a shame and guilt filled him that he didn't know could exist, as he thought about how his grandpa was probably rolling over in his grave right now. Out of pure hatred for the black race and this nigger named Tommy Good. Haywood Jefferson wanted to say something in response to the way

Tommy treated him, but he knew better. It was something deadly about the man, plus he paid him too well.

"I'm sure it was Mr. Good."

"Did you go out back to the chicken coop and feed my chickens?" Tommy asked.

"Yes sir. I even tried to feed the black crow in the cage in the living room, but it attacked me," Mr. Jefferson said and Tommy smiled. He knew Aunt Ertha hated white people even more than he did, especially growing up down there in the south where she saw slavery firsthand.

"Yeah, I should've warned you about that bird. Leave her alone. I'll tend to it," Tommy told him and headed into the living room where the huge gold cage sat directly under a chandelier.

"Hey Mr. Jefferson," Lady said following Tommy into the house. "Don't pay him no mind," she said sympathetically to the old white man.

"That's nice of you to say Ms. Lady."

Aunt Ertha flapped her wings wildly as she sat perched on the stand inside the bird cage the moment she saw Tommy enter the room. She had been in the soul of this bird's belly since the day she lost her life of the human flesh performing her last mojo job to give Tommy back life, and she didn't regret it one bit. It was well worth it to her because she passed on more than life to Tommy. She gave him the art, the art of witchcraft and the power of voodoo. Tommy was now a tainted soul who gave his life to the devil.

"Hey Aunt Ertha!" Tommy said happily at the sight of the crow with the head full of white feathers. The bird let off a high pitched "squawk" of approval as Tommy opened the cage. He grabbed a leather shoulder cover used for the bird to perch itself on and tossed it over his left shoulder, then let Aunt Ertha walk up his arm and nestle her claws into the shoulder pad. He dug his hand down into the bird feed and grabbed a handful of cashews as the bird ate out of the palm of his hand. Watching Aunt Ertha eat the cashews, Tommy thought back on the day he died and realized just how lucky he was to have Aunt Ertha.

It just wasn't something right about these two niggaz that walked up asking for weed, and Tommy felt it. Not wanting to overreact, he played it cool.

"Ain't nuffin but dope and crack sold on this block my man," Tommy told the one who asked for some weed then it all happened in a blur.

The first of the two started throwing the knives, killing one of Tommy and Mike's young boys instantly. Then the other one unloaded with a round of shots from both the guns he held, catching Tommy with several shots. It was then that the man appeared staring down at him. The last thing he remembered was the fire that spat from the barrel ending his life. "Imma kill Pretty E's ass!"

Chapter Three

Courtroom 6A at the New Castle County Superior Court on 5th and King St. was jam-packed to its capacity. So much so that people stood in the aisles and against the back wall, all trying to see the outcome of the trial everyone was talking about. The trial of Tammy Washington's attempted murder case on her ex-boyfriend Eric "Pretty E" Williams. All week long person after person from the club the night of the shooting testified and pointed the finger at Tammy, who sat at the defense table in a red prison suit from Baylor's Women Correctional Institute. Today, though would be the most powerful testimony of them all, the testimony of Pretty E.

"All rise!" the bailiff yelled out over the courtroom, "the honorable Judge Evans presiding."

"You may be seated. State, call your next witness," the Judge ordered.

"Yes your Honor. The State of Delaware would like to call Eric Williams," the prosecutor stated, and the courtroom fell silent. This was the day everyone present in the courtroom came to see. The day they brought Pretty E into the courthouse, there were so many rumors and speculations floating around about Pretty E, it was pathetic. Some said he was a vegetable, others said he was paralyzed and wheelchair bound, and some even said he was dead. Today though, all would see the man, the legend, the myth in full color once he walked into the courtroom.

When the doors to courtroom 6A opened in the rear of the courtroom, every head in attendance turned to see Pretty E, even Tammy at the defense table. Accompanied by his fiancé, Egypt and their newborn son, Rasul Hakeem, named after Rasul and Hit Man. Pretty E was still pretty as ever. Only thing was he now walked with a cane. The bullets from Tammy's gun that night slightly paralyzed his left side. The onlookers were impressed to say the least. Dressed in Farragamo with a silk tie and quarter cut ostrich and gator boot, Pretty E lived up to his name, while flashing his pearly white, freshly cleaned thirty-twos at some of the familiar faces. Led by the bailiff, Pretty E was escorted to the stand.

"State your name," the prosecutor said.

"Eric Williams."

"Hi Mr. Williams. Can I call you Eric?"

"Yes," he answered.

"Is that a cane I seen you walking with?"

"Yes."

"May I ask why?"

"I was shot several times in the chest and abdomen at my club some months ago."

"Yes, I've heard, as did the jurors of this trial. It is to my and the courtrooms knowledge that Ms. Tammy Washington is responsible for your condition. Is that right?"

"I object your Honor!" the defense shouted.

"You may proceed."

"Eric do you see Ms. Tammy Washington in this courtroom today?"

"Yes, she's right there in the red prison clothes," Pretty E said and made eye contact with Tammy for the first time in almost a year. Instantly when their eyes met, Pretty E realized just how much he still had love for the woman who had been with him since the day they met on South St. at Dr. Denim's in Philly. This was the same woman that carried his drugs across the Mexican border and over the seas that separated the U.S.A. from Colombia. The same woman that time and time again proved her love for him only to be betrayed by him and one of his many white women, mainly Lucy and Monique. This was the same woman that drugged him and threw hot water on him all out of love for him. Now, this was the same woman on trial for trying to kill him. With their eyes still locked deep into one another's, Tammy, with tears in her eyes, mouthed the words "I'm sorry Eric," and "I love you." Pretty E read her lips clearly and shot her a wink and nod that only she caught, then he tapped his chest where his heart was.

"Eric do you also see the person in this courtroom that shot you today?" and Pretty E began to let his eyes go over the courtroom.

"No. The person who shot me isn't here," he said and a loud gasp could be heard throughout the courtroom. Pretty E's answer shocked them all.

"Are you certain Mr. Williams?"

"As sure as that's my name ma'am," Pretty E said, and Tammy let out a sigh of relief.

"Prosecution rests."

"Defense has nothing further," and in less than ten minutes, the weeklong trial was determined. Tammy was found "Not Guilty". On his way out the door, Pretty E was approached by Monique looking good as ever. She stopped in front of him and Egypt and thanked him from the bottom of her heart, which really pissed Egypt off even more.

■■■■■

"What da fuck was that all about?" Egypt scorned through slit eyes. "What? You still fucking da bitch?!"

"What are you talking about Egypt? Calm down baby," he told her noticing the crowd of onlookers that switched their attention to the arguing couple.

"Calm down?! Calm down?!"

How can you ask me that after you just let the bitch that tried to kill you walk?! How am I supposed to feel? I mean she almost took you away from me, almost left me a single mother, and your son a bastard child. So calm down is the last thing I'm going to do Eric! What?! Do you still love Tammy or something?" she asked, and he took a little too long for her to answer, so she started to turn away. "Just like I thought," Egypt spoke with tears and black eyeliner rolling down her face. "I knew you would never change. I'm such a fucking fool!" she said throwing her hands up in the air talking to whoever was listening. That's when she realized something; she wasn't carrying her son, and stopped dead in her tracks.

"Give me my son! I'll be damned if he turns out like you!" Egypt was still going off, only this time in front of a capacity of people. She reached Pretty E, snatched her son away, and walked off fast.

18

"Egypt! Egypt!" Pretty E called out to his first love, but she didn't stop. "Egypt!" he yelled again. This time she stopped.

"What?!" she snapped, and when she turned around all she could do was cover her mouth with the hand not holding the baby. Pretty E was down on one knee, braced up against his cane and holding out in his hand a ring the size of a "lima bean".

"Baby will you marry me?"

"Yes I'll marry you dummy!" Egypt said and ran into his awaiting arms nearly smashing Rasul Hakeem. He laughed a gummy smile at the sudden position he was in between his parents causing them to laugh too, and the crowd of onlookers to cheer.

■■■■■■

Later that night outside of Deloris Baylor Women's Correctional Institute, Tammy was being released for a second time. Her girlfriend and new love of her life was waiting outside like she knew she would be. There wasn't a doubt in her mind. Just as sure as the jury found her "Not Guilty", Monique was right outside parked in the Benz.

"Welcome home baby!" Monique greeted Tammy and the two of them never made it out of the prison parking lot. They made love right there in the back seat of the car, while the whole time Tammy thought, "Eric baby it's not over, you'll always be mine! Or nobody's at all," she smirked as her cum ran down Monique's chin.

"Mmm-Mmm delicious!" Monique said. "I mean good."

"Like Campbell soup baby!" Tammy responded with a smile as they continued their sex with a mean body fuck.

Chapter Four

Today was Friday, the beginning of Raven's weekend. She didn't have any more classes until Tuesday morning, so to prepare for her four-day weekend; she pulled out her Blackberry Touch from Verizon and scrolled through her task and memos on her phone. Seeing that she had nothing visible to do, she decided on spending some time with Big Mom, Tommy's grandmother.

Raven drove her Beemer down 9th Street, the street Tommy ran and turned on Pine St. so she could come up Poplar St. When she turned onto 10th Street, just like she figured there wasn't a parking spot in sight. Luckily, she saw "Nardo" one of Tommy's little cousin's, leaving Big Mom's with Sheem, his right hand man.

"What's up Raven? What chu stopping by to see Big Mom?" he asked.

"Yeah, why? She in there right?"

"Yeah, she in there."

"Why it ain't never no place to park around here?" she asked herself more so than Nardo, but he offered his help anyway.

"Yo, I'll park it for you. Plus I do need to use it right quick, huh Sheem?"

"Yeah, we could use it right quick Raven," Sheem added and looked at Raven who he had a crush on for years. From the day Tommy first brought her around, Nardo and Sheem both had eyes for Tommy's new girl, but knew it was out of the question.

"For what?" she asked throwing it in park in the middle of the street. "I know y'all don't think y'all dropping some drugs off in my shit, do y'all?"

"No, no. It ain't nuffin' like that. We just want to holla at these two broads right quick."

"Who? What lil stank hoes y'all trying to put in my car?"

"Some broads named Boochie and Brooklyn," Nardo said.

"Ain't they some Dyke broads or some um?" Raven asked, hearing those names somewhere before.

"Nah," Sheem said, they go both ways.

"What time are y'all bringing my car back?" she asked looking at her Gucci watch that read 6:00 p.m.

"In a couple hours," Nardo and Sheem said in unison.

"Damn, the least y'all can do is carry Tommy Jr. and the car seat in the house," Raven said, noticing the traffic starting to back up on the street.

"Oh, I ain't even see him in there," Nardo said and carried him and the seat in the house. "We out," he said brushing by Raven.

"And fill my shit up or you won't use that again," she promised.

"Gotchu cousin!" Nardo hollered back and he and Sheem pulled off.

Raven walked into Big Mom's house and instantly felt the love. It was just something about Big Mom's house, all grandmothers' houses for that matter that sent off a feeling of comfort, love, safety, and security. The thing that really made it feel like a home though was the aroma that was coming out of the kitchen. And to anyone familiar with black family households, you already knew what it was on this Friday. You got damn right! Fish, fried potatoes, baked beans with plenty of cinnamon and sugar, and applesauce.

"Hey Big Mom! We didn't impose on you did we?" Raven asked walking into the living room to find her taking Little Tommy's over clothes off of him and pulling him from the car seat.

"No chile, Big Mom wasn't doing nuffin but watching her shows. You know I needs my Jeopardy, Wheel of Fortune, and my numbers," she began.

"So how you been doing Big Mom?"

"Oh, Big Mom has been fine. It's you youngins I need to be asking how it is that y'all are doing. Shoot— it's so bad out there now Big Mom don't know what to do. I'm scared to walk down to Bennie's Big Scoop nowadays, and you know that used to be my exercise I even gotta lock my door now chile. I ain't ever had to lock my doors for nuffin!! If I don't them damn jug heads, vase heads, whateva y'all call'em been done came up in here and took all Big Mom's stuff."

"Are you talking about base heads Big Mom?"

"Yea dat's them! I'm so glad we got 'ol Barack in office chile, I don't know what to do?! I know he better make some changes and fast or it's going to be some mad black folk out here!!" she thought about the new Black and only Black President the United States of America ever elected. It was a day and time she never thought she'd live to see in her lifetime, but she did, and she remembered that day in Nov. 08 like it was yesterday. The day the world watched history be made and America elect Mr. Barack Hussein Obama as the H.N.I.C. "Hallelujah!" Big Mom screamed and shouted and cried at the same time. To her and every other elderly black person whom, like Big Mom was around to see the late depression, the beginning of segregation, the assassination of Kennedy, and now this. They each felt as though their vote and entire day of prayer made it happen.

"You ain't lying Big Mom!!"

"I know I ain't chile," Big Mom said and looked at Raven seriously. "So how are you doing? Did you meet you somebody yet?

I know you're tired of being in that big' ol house down there by yourself. Girl you better find you someone to grow old with. You ain't going to be young forever," she said matter-of-factly.

"Big Mom, I am good. I'm fine with me and Little Tommy."

"Chile, you know what I mean. We women have needs that only a man can meet if you know what I'm talking about," Big Mom paused then continued, "you know your pudding can dry up and close on you right?" Big Mom chuckled.

"Big Mooom!" Raven said, shocked at Big Mom's choice of words.

"Chile I'm just kidding wit' chu. Big Mom felt like a little laugh. Seriously though, it will turn gray down there. But that ain't nuffin, wait till it goes bald," she laughed again. "Here chile, take this baby for a minute," Big Mom said and walked over to the china cabinet and grabbed an old framed picture. Raven smiled on that note, as she thought about how black people knew they could use something for what it's not. Like now, that china cabinet never had a dish.

"See this baby? This was Big Mom when I was your age. Now look at me," she said with her arms outstretched. "What you need to do is get out there and finds you a man chile because Tommy ain't coming back. That's my only regret," Big Mom continued, "I never married again after my husband died. Now I gotta grow old and die by myself. No one wants to die alone."

Raven held the picture of Big Mom in her hand and stared at the beautiful woman she once was. She looked up to the lady she was now and the only resemblance she saw was the eyes. Big Mom still had those bright doe eyes. Raven knew that everything Big Mom was saying to her was true like always because Big Mom never held a punch. Whether it hurt Raven or not she always told her the truth like now. Tommy wasn't coming back.

"What you need to do is stop trying to compare everybody you meet to Tommy and give one of these nice gentlemen out here a chance. Cause if you keep on comparing you'll never find a man cause ain't nare none of them going to match up. Baby, Tommy was one of a kind," Big Mom smiled at the thought of her favorite grandbaby of them all. And like always it was as if Big Mom had read her mind. Big Mom, all Big Mom's from all over the world each held that canniness and knowledge of nearly everything. There wasn't a place that they lacked. They held all job positions of life. They were mothers, fathers, babysitters, chefs, disciplinarians, educators, doctors, storytellers, you name it, and they became it. Big Mom was that rare breed of human beings that was nearly extinct in today's society because the Big Mom's of today were barely pushing 40. So as long as Raven had this Big Mom, the Big Mom with the slide-on slippers, polyester pants, wig, and apron, she was going to spend as much time with her as she could. Because when she went on to pass away she'd be gravely missed.

"I know Big Mom. I do need to give somebody a chance. It's just, I haven't really been looking," she told the truth. She had started lusting though, she couldn't help it because people told her to move on so much all she thought about was men here lately. If it wasn't Ann, it was her sister Robin. If it wasn't Mia, Uncle Bear's old girl who just recently married and became an Evangelist for the church, it was Big Mom. "Damn! They worried about me getting some more than I am," she thought and in walked Nardo and Sheem.

"What's up Big Mom," they both greeted their favorite lady.

"Here are your keys Raven," Nardo said and handed them to her.

"So did y'all see Boochie and Brooklyn?"

"Yeah we saw 'em."

"Well why y'all needed my car to go see 'em. Don't they got cars? Or shit, y'all could've drove y'alls own cars," Raven said, still not quite understanding why they needed hers.

"Nah we wasn't driving our shits. Those bitches are gold diggers. Wasn't no way I was letting them broads see me pushing my 745 CLS. They would've really had they hand out. Shit, they already wanted a stack a piece!" Sheem answered.

"Eeeew! I know y'all didn't go out trickin'?"

"It ain't trickin' if you got it!!" Nardo said.

"Let me find out!" Raven said and started gathering her and Tommy Jr.'s things. Tonight she had gotten an earful from Big Mom and needed to go lie down and digest it. "Come to think of it, I do miss being cuddled up next to a man," she thought as Nardo and Sheem walked her to her car. "Bye Big Mom!"

"See ya chile."

Chapter Five

Ann rolled over in bed only to find Mike not there, so she sat up. Listening for any sounds that could be heard she keened in on all her other senses, and there was nothing. She couldn't smell anything cooking, she didn't hear the shower, and even the kids were silent; that made her get up and go check their room. They weren't there. "I wonder where they're at?" she thought about the men in her life. "And I know damn well he ain't forget that today was our anniversary," she spoke out loud. This was the first time since they started messing around at Tommy's block party when they were twelve that Mike hadn't greeted her with a "Happy Anniversary — Annie Fannie," and she was shocked. Little did she know, this would be her best anniversary as of yet.

Mike got out of bed this morning as softly and quietly as he possibly could. He crept down the hallway to his son's room and woke them just as quietly and got them dressed. He had a "hell-a" morning in front of him if he wanted everything to go smoothly as planned. "Come on y'all. I'm taking y'all to school today," Mike said to the boys.

"Why? Where mommy at?" they asked.

"She sleep, now come on," he said. He didn't want to take no chances on waking Ann up and spoiling everything he had planned.

Once Mike had dropped the kids off at school, his day of a total make over begun. His first stop was at the barber shop to get his haircut down to a "1" against the grain with a mean line-up and all his facial hairs shaven off. Next he drove to the tailor and picked up his one of a kind, specially made suit with black Louis Vuitton fabric that he paid a grip for. And lastly, he drove to the limousine service to pick up the black stretch Cadillac D.T.S. When all of that was complete and he was dressed for the surprise anniversary present he had lined up for Ann, he called his two young boys from off the 9 and told them to be ready. He then called his boy cool ass Dave from back in the "boys' chase the girls" and "hide and go get it" days and told him he was ready. Cool ass Dave was a state police officer now, and he was going to have a convoy of squad cars give the limousine a police escort all the way to his house.

Mike had the limousine driver drive to the eastside from the limousine service and pull up on 9th St. Like he expected, his two young boys to be, they were dressed like two CIA agents equipped with walkie-talkies and the whole nine yards.

"Come on y'all get in," Mike told them as they sat in the limo awaiting the police escort from the Delaware State Police. "It's Showtime," Mike thought when he heard the sirens nearing.

■■■■■■

"Oh my God Victor, watch out! The bitch got a gun!" Ann yelled at the T.V. as she stuffed some Pringles in her mouth after taking a big bite of her roast beef sandwich. "Young and the Restless" was her shit and in no way did she want Victor Newman's ex-wife Nikki to shoot him in the back when she snuck in his office. On the edge of her couch, mouth wide open from mid-chew, she yelled at the T.V. again, but to no avail. "Pow! Pow!" the shots sounded and Victor fell into the bookcase. Then she heard the sirens. "Well damn, these muthafuckin stories getting realer than real," she smiled hearing the sirens right after the gun shots. Then she got off the couch to see what all the commotion was about. It seemed like the cops were right outside her door.

"What da fuck?" Ann said to herself when she saw all the police cars outside of her house.

■■■■■■

Never moving from behind the curtain and staring out, Ann watched as the state police officers formed a line up to her door on both sides of her sidewalk. Next, the limousine driver who stood at the back door of the limo opened it up and two look-a-like CIA agents got out followed by another man. Instantly all of the officers went into salute position as the man carrying the little American flag walked between them. It wasn't until the man got right up on the door than she knew who it was. "It's Mike, but what is he up to?" she thought as he knocked on the door.

"Yes," she answered when she opened the door.

"Hello Mrs. Cottman," Mike began and gave her the hand held flag. "I'm Mr. Barack Obama, and I came personally to thank you for your vote. It was your vote that got me in office," he said, and Ann was flabbergasted. She instantly caught on and fell right in place. Mike was role-playing, something she loved to do for him.

"I'm speechless Mr. President," Ann said still not believing everything her husband went through to make her anniversary this special. "What do I do next? I'm at a loss for words."

"Well you can invite me in for starters," he told her and she backed away from the entrance of the door to let him in.

"Have a seat. Would you like something to drink?" Ann asked him as she led him to the couch.

"No, I'm good," Mike responded with his eyes glued on Ann's backside.

"Mr. President!" she said catching him. "What about Michele Obama? I would never want to hurt my sistah!"

"What your sistah don't know won't hurt her," he responded and took Ann into his arms.

Over the next 45 minutes or so, instead of exploring the oval office of the white office, Mike explored the oval office of his wife's body. And just like every time they had sex, it was like the first time they had sex. Mike and Ann couldn't get enough of each other.

"My God Mr. President!" Ann called out as she came yet another time. "Your almost as good as my husband!"

"Your husband?!" Mike asked bewildered.

"Yeah my husband. But I'll never tell," she smiled and winked.

"Happy Anniversary — Annie Fannie!" Mike said and they shared a long passionate kiss.

Chapter Six

For today to be Christmas morning, it couldn't have been going more fucked up for Jaquan than it was. In the last two weeks he had lost one of his gunners Snotty, and Kyle was just all the way fucked up. He couldn't see, talk, or nothing. His heart went out to him. Now this, he just received a call that said last night Greeny and his son were found in their house burnt to a crisp. "Damn!" he thought, but that's how the cookie crumbled. You do dirt, you get dirt. And Greeny, Snotty, and Kyle had done so much dirt to people; it could've been anyone that offed them. The police investigation was at a standstill. Then to top it all off, Jaquan couldn't get his hands on no cocaine at all!! Damn, drought season was a muthafucka!

"You mean to tell me you couldn't find no blow?" Jaquan asked as he sat in his uncle's, Pretty E's, office at "Hood Concrete" leaned back in the seat with his Prada sneaks propped up on the edge of the desk as he talked to O.D.B. "Not even like 10 of them things?" Jaquan asked unbelievingly.

"Man I couldn't find nuffin. The only place I know of right now that's a "Go" is down the Dirty South. I called my cousin "Lil Biscuit", Biz for short, and he said it's a nigga down there that got it like snow on the ground," O.D.B. told him.

"Where dis at? And who dis nigga posed to be?"

"Down New Orleans, and the nigga'z name is "Reno"."

"Reno?" Jaquan said as more of a question to himself. "I think I heard that name somewhere before."

"Yeah dem cash money niggaz, I mean Chopper City Boys be shouting him out in them songs."

"Oh yeah! That's the nigga B.G. and Juvie be talking bout."

"Yeah, that's him."

"Well do Biz know this nigga?"

"Yeah. Said he fuck with him like that, like that. My auntie and 'em said Biz is doing some thangs for his self," O.D.B. assured his best friend. Every since Boog came up missing he's been Jaquan's right hand man.

"So what's up? You trying to pay your cousin Biz a visit?" Jaquan asked him and in walked Pretty E.

"Damn right," O.D.B. said.

"Get ya feet off my desk lil nigga," Pretty E said and playfully smacked Jaquan's Prada's off of it.

"Damn, it's like dat Unc?" Jaquan teased, but out of respect didn't put his feet back up on the desk.

"So what's up? What you two niggaz talking about?" Pretty asked them.

"Nuffin really. We trying to get our hands on some blow dat all. This drought got a nigga missing some "meals" feel me?"

"You need to be glad it's a drought right now. Both of y'all do. This is the time you get to sit back and re-evaluate some things, you dig? Nigga, y'all are already up. I know for a fact them suits (Feds) is watching because I see them following me everyday almost. Thing is, niggaz can't touch me. I'm clean as the board of health. Now you two lil niggaz is who I'm worried about. What y'all need to do is fall back, let this thing blow over, then decide on what y'all want to do," Pretty E lectured them.

"All that shit sounds good Unc, but did you, my pop, Uncle Dog, and Uncle Hit Man stop when it was a drought?" Pretty E couldn't answer him. "That's what I thought," Jaquan said and in walked Pretty E's new secretary.

"Mr. Eric, here's your coffee. It's just like you like it. Plenty sugar and a whole lot of cream. It's almost as white as me," Brooke said with a giggle. She knew Pretty E had a thing for her. She knew this because on more than one occasion they had flirted with one another. They even shared a few passionate kisses.

"And you know I like that," Pretty E shot back as he watched the "Blonde Beauty" with the ass-length hair walk out of the office. All three of them stared. Brooke was definitely a "playmate".

"That's what you need to re-evaluate because Aunt Egypt ain't having that shit!" Jaquan said.

"Man that girl types 65 words per minute!" Pretty E exclaimed and they fell out laughing.

"Just like Lucy and Monique" Jaquan said.

For the next hour, Jaquan and O.D.B. talked about life, sports, and women. With Pretty E, along with his thoughts about the trip down to the N.O, they went over every possible scenario, from prices down to transporting, and when they were finished, they had it all planned out. O.D.B. would make the first trip by himself to meet the plug, but when it was time to cop, Jaquan would be going along. So after it was all set, Pretty E and Brooke called and booked the flight for O.D.B.

■■■■■■

Raven had just walked through the front door when her house phone rang. She looked at the caller ID and smiled, it was her brother Jaquan. "He probably wants to say Merry Christmas knowing we don't celebrate holidays being as though we're Muslims," she said to herself, but had to admit all the lights and shit outside did put you in the holiday spirit.

"Hello," she answered on the fifth ring.

"Hello. Damn girl—what took you so long to get the phone?" Jaquan asked.

"I just walked in the door."

"Oh. Where my nephew at?"

"Right here."

"You got a babysitter?"

"Why?"

"Because I'm trying to go up Philly to the new strip club, Onyx. You wit it?"

"Eeew boy no! What I look like going to a strip club to watch some bitches dance naked?"

"Nah see it ain't even like that. This mufuckin strip joint here is like the ones down the "ATL". It be men and women up in dat piece. It's like a regular club," Jaquan told her.

"I don't know. Let me think about it."

"Man, I'll be there at 10 o'clock," Jaquan told her.

"Ok, damn! At least let me try to find a babysitter," Raven said.

"Yeah, tell 'em I got a couple hundred for the night."

"Aight, let me call Ann," she said and hung up the phone.

Finding a babysitter was the least of Raven's worries, she had them at her disposal. Trying to decide if she really wanted to go out was the thing. She had only been out twice before since the death of Tommy and once after Tommy Jr. was born. Each time she got nothing out of it. It was the same old shit. "Hey baby what's your name?" "Can I buy you a drink?" "Damn, you sexy as hell! Anybody ever tell you that?" and all kinds of other lame shit. To be truthful, Raven hated that shit. Why did all niggaz think that hanging on to some negative street code bullshit would earn them brownie points? Don't no real woman find that cool shit attractive. Niggaz really needed to grow up. It was 2010!!

After making up her mind, confirming the babysitting with Ann, and getting dressed, she sat and waited on both Ann and Jaquan to come. Ann got there first being as though she only lived minutes away from Pike Creek in Hockessin, but she refused to leave without seeing her young boy crush, Jaquan. And although that's all it was, Ann knew that in another day and lifetime, she would've fucked his little sexy ass to death!!

"When he say he was coming?" Ann asked Raven for the umpteenth time.

"He said 10 o'clock. Girl, you is crazy! You better leave my big brother alone."

"Girl I ain't going to mess with your brother, I only want to lust a little bit. You know I would never cheat on my husband girl. All of us would be dead," she said with a laugh, but was dead serious. Mike would have surely killed them all.

At 10 o'clock on the dot both Raven and Ann heard the knock on the front door. "Dere go my baby!" Ann blushed as Raven went to get the door. "Girl shut up," Raven said over her shoulder knowing Ann was joking. However, there was a lot of truth in a joke.

"Damn, aren't we prompt and on time?" Raven said to her brother who stood before her looking like a star athlete or some shit.

"I'm always punctual baby sis, all the way down to my shoe strings," he said and stepped back so she could get a full look.

"I guess," she said, but had to admit that her brother was definitely that nigga!

Dressed in a loose fitting pair of black Gucci jeans, sneaks, and a sweater to match, with a full-length mink to fit his 6'6" frame the color of the sky, Jaquan looked just like who he was: "MONEY".

"You guess what lil sis?" he said and ran his huge hand over his "Freeway" like beard, conditioned and greased up with "Shea butter". "Hey sexy don't I know you?" Jaquan said to Ann flirting, something they did after the second time they met. Ann blushed. Just looking at this man who stood 6'6" tall with a caramel complexion, a head full of waves, and size 13 sneaks, made Ann realize that there were other men in the hood that she could be attracted to.

"Yes you do know me. Now come give me my hug like always so I can get my lust and free fills on," Ann said and stood up, and the two embraced. "Mmmm" Ann

37

moaned softly then said, "Boy if I wasn't married I'd give you some of this good pussy, even though you are a baby. How old are you again, twenty-one?" she asked.

"Age ain't nuffin but a number."

"Ok, Ok, Ok! That's enough!!" Raven said, breaking the two from their embrace. "It's time to go Jaquan and Ann. Y'all are going to make us late and I'm a change my mind."

When Jaquan let Ann go, she tapped him on the butt and winked. She made a mental note right then and there to leave well enough alone because for the first time in her life, her pussy throbbed for someone else.

"So why'd you ask me to go to the strip club with you? Where's O.D.B.?"

"He had to make a run down south right quick," Jaquan told his sister as they pulled off in his Maybach Coupe. Like Jay-Z said, "I'm still spending money from '88," and so was Jaquan. He was spending his stepfather, Rasul's money. Jaquan looked to the sky like he often did and said, "Thanks pops," as they turned onto I-95 North.

Chapter Seven

The flight from the Philadelphia International Airport to Shreveport, Louisiana International took four hours and fifteen minutes. Chewing on a half a pack of Big Red chewing gum to keep his ears from popping, O.D.B. stepped off the plane and headed into the airport to baggage claims. It seemed as if nothing had changed about the airport since he was last there nearly 10 years ago. So he wasn't lost at all. He used to take this same flight every summer of his life up until his 14th birthday when he was tired of coming down the south to meet and stay with his father's side of the family. Now it was a different story. O.D.B. was down here for straight business.

Wheeling his Louis Vuitton luggage on its roller wheels through the airport, O.D.B. was reminded it was Christmas by the people singing carols' throughout the airport. Being from up North, it was easy to forget when the weather in the South was in its seventies as opposed to the twenties and thirties up North. Recognizing the huge change in the weather, O.D.B. shed the leather Louis V. coat with the snorkel hood he was wearing and folded and smashed it into his biggest suit case. It was just too hot for the coat he reasoned. So there he stood outside in the terminal looking like just a regular patron waiting for his ride in his Coogi sweater, jeans, and fresh pair of construction Tims. It wasn't until you saw the huge bracelet and watch on both his wrists that you knew he wasn't the average Joe. Those two pieces of jewelry by Jacob the Jeweler Co. had the diamonds in them dancing like the sun sparkling on Lake Michigan on a bright sunny day. O.D.B. couldn't help but admire the way people stared at his two pieces, and they should when they grand totaled one hundred and forty thousand dollars.

"Are you a rapper?" one woman in her mid-thirties asked him.

"Nah, I'm an entrepreneur," he told her, then noticed the hottest "Dunk" he ever saw.

"Lil Biscuit", O.D.B.'s cousin earned that name because as a child he needed to have a biscuit with everything he ate. It didn't matter how the biscuit was, sweet potato, cheese, or covered in syrup, he had to have one. "Biz" as he was known for short was only six months younger than O.D.B., so they grew up together every summer. It had been almost 10 years since he last saw him, and he couldn't wait to reunite with his favorite cousin from up North. The last time they spoke on the phone, they filled each other in on bits and pieces of their lives, but didn't go into much detail because they were on cell phones. In the line of work they were in, they knew better than to talk on them. They saw the "Feds" bring down whole crime families by tapping phones, and they weren't going to be indicted on nothing as a result of a phone and meant that shit. So they talked in code and kept it short and sweet.

♫ *Like A Stripper*
Up And Down Like Flipper

Bend Over
Let Me See It From Da Back

Webbie's: "Like A Stripper"

Lil Webbie's "Like a Stripper" pounded through the composition system by Rockford Fossgate that Biz had put in his '79 Cutlass. Sitting high on a double lift kit, and a pair of 26" rims, the Cutlass looked wet. The Jolly Rancher Green candy paint that looked as if it would drip did nothing but compliment the all white guts piped in green with "Biz" etched in the headrests. This particular "Dunk" was Biz's favorite although it wasn't his favorite car. He had a 2010 Camaro that was his pet. Biz let his foot off the pedal as soon as he entered the terminal and cruised slowly up to Delta Airlines gates. He slammed on the brakes and jumped out the minute he seen his cousin Omar standing there with his luggage. With the door open and the music still pounding the terminal like a block party, Biz yelled, "Say bruh you need a ride?"

"Oh shit! Is dat you nigga?" O.D.B. said rushing to embrace his cousin he hadn't seen in years.

"Who else can it be folk?"

"Damn! You ain't change a bit, got a lil chubby that's all."

"Naw nigga dis he'ah good living bruh," Biz said and rubbed his pot belly. "Yea a nigga ol' lady keeps them meals coming."

"Who is she?"

"You going meet her folk and you ain't going believe yo eyes bruh. Shit going trip you out fo'real," he spoke like a true "Nawlins" person, and then they were interrupted by the terminal security.

"Y'all are going to have to move this along," the officer said.

"Say bruh, can us folk load our shit first my nigga? Damn! Go fuck wit dem white folk right dere, they been here longer than us."

"Chill Biz," O.D.B. said. He didn't want to make no enemies, especially not here at the airport.

"Naw bruh, dat's some fuck shit!" Biz said still offended by the officer.

"Don't worry about it. Let's just load this luggage and bounce," O.D.B. said and tossed one of the cases in the cars backseat.

With the luggage packed and them settled in the "Dunk", Biz left the airport and hopped on I-10 East towards New Orleans. O.D.B. couldn't help but notice the way the engine purred as they cruised the Interstate. From the rumble of the engine O.D.B. knew Biz had something under the hood so he tested him.

"Nigga, what you got underneath the hood?"

"A 484 bruh!"

"Man, dis shit still slow," O.D.B. challenged him.

"Oh yeah? Say bruh, hold on!" and Biz punched the gas.

O.D.B. couldn't believe how fast they were going in a matter of seconds. This was the best Cutlass he ever rode in. Even with all the extras, the Cutlass still rode luxurious while packing the power of a Vette. He knew then that he wanted a toy just like this.

"Ok, ok cuz! Slow dis mufucka down!" O.D.B. pleaded.

"Say bruh, I know you ain't hoeing up over dere?" Biz laughed.

"Nah, I just feel safer when I'm behind the wheel at these speeds," and Biz slowed down. He knew exactly what his cousin meant, because he ain't like to be in cars with a nigga speeding either. "So what's up with granny?"

"She good folk. She going end up out living all of us. She can't wait to see you. You know she been up all last night getting that Christmas dinner together. Oh and guess what bruh?"

"What?"

"She made your favorite; sweet shortening bread and cookies. Wouldn't even let nobody taste um. Said these he'ah is for Omar!" Biz mocked his grand mom and O.D.B. smiled. He couldn't wait to see the ol' lady.

■■■■■■

Biz hit the N.O. in no time. Living in the Holly Grove section of the city made it even shorter of a ride from the airport because it was right off the exit. He turned and made a left onto his street and drove halfway down the block before he was turning into his driveway. Biz lived with his girl Janelle, who they used to call J.J. as a child in an expensive, but modest three bed room home newly renovated. Outside in the driveway sat another pink "Dunk" identical to Biz's green one, his Camaro, and his show car. A Pepsi blue "68" '98 Oldsmobile with the guts the same color dark blue as a Pepsi, while the seats were stitched with white nylon the same color as its convertible top. Sitting on "30s", the car could have passed for a monster truck.

"Now that mufucka there! Now that's hot!" O.D.B. said excitedly.

"Yeah my nigga. Cream on da inside, clean on da outside! Ice, ice, ice, ice, ice cream paint job!" he sung the chorus to a song that was killing the air waves. "Come on bruh. Let's go get you settled in."

Janelle was out on the back deck with her best friend Tamia, smoking a vanilla dutchie when she heard them pull up. She had been telling her about Omar every since he said he was coming down today, and she was surely trying to hook the two of them up. "Who else better for my boy than my home girl," she thought remembering back to the days her and Omar were inseparable.

Janelle met Omar (O.D.B.), the first summer he visited New Orleans when they were both just six years old. And from the day they met on the sidewalk racing big wheels, till the time the summer was over, they shadowed each other. Janelle was a tomboy who at six was rougher than him and Lil Biscuit. She threw rocks, played sandlot football with them, basketball, and went fishing. She and O.D.B. had become so close that Biz would get jealous and the two of them, Janelle and Biz, would come to blows. The two of them couldn't stand each other and wouldn't speak all year long until the following summer when Omar would come back. That's why it blew his mind when he hit the back deck and saw J.J. come running.

"Omar! Omar! Omar!" she gleamed and ran straight towards O.D.B.

"Daaaamn girl look at you!" he said and held her out at arm's length. He couldn't believe how much this little flat-chested, tight butt tomboy he remembered as J.J. had turned into a lady.

"I know huh, folk?" she said and ran her hands all over her curvaceous body. "But look at you! All grown up and shit," she said looking at how much Omar had changed. He looked good as shit with his smooth dark chocolate skin, and full beard like Bin Laden's. Big beards were the shit up North because it represented your faith in Allah and you being a Sunni Muslim. However, some dudes think it's a fashion or fad. So please if you're not Muslim, cut that shit off!! You give the true Muslims a bad name.

"Yeah it ain't bout nuffin," he responded.

"Hey baby," she said to Biz and went to kiss him on the lips, then introduced O.D.B. and Tamia. "Omar, this is Tamia my best friend."

"Hey, what's up baby girl?" O.D.B. asked her causing her to blush at his accent.

"Nuffin. Been sitting here for hours waiting to meet you," Tamia said honestly.

"Was I worth the wait?"

"I don't know yet. It's still too early to tell," she said and looked up into his eyes. O.D.B. was stuck.

Tamia Valdez was a twenty-three year old Creole woman who cheer leaded for the New Orleans Saints and Hornets. And from her beauty it was hard to imagine her doing anything else but modeling or cheering, and marrying one of those million dollar athletes, but she was different. Tamia didn't let the fact that her beauty was unmatchable to nearly everyone she encountered change her from being that same humble and modest person into becoming a self-centered, arrogant bitch, although it would have been understandable. Beautiful people of the world all sent off that arrogance in some way or another, but the conceited bug didn't bite her. Which was hard to believe if you ever seen a Creole woman. Creole women were beautiful. Being of French decent and Haitian, the mixture gave Creole women the Island look. They almost looked white, but they were black with ocean blue eyes and wavy hair like a Hispanic. To sum Tamia all up in one word would be "Pocahontas". The girl was just that beautiful.

"Too early to tell? Well I'm here all week that should be plenty of time."

"We'll see," she shot back. It was something about him she liked.

"I'm glad to see y'all two are hitting it off," Janelle said when she came back to the deck carrying a bottle of Grey Goose, some pineapple juice, and some glasses.

"Yeah we aight," Tamia said with a smile. Janelle knew she approved of her match-making.

"So what's up for tonight? What we doing babe?" Janelle asked Biz as she poured everyone drinks.

"Well I know we going to the "Rodeo Show" fo'sho, because I gotta introduce my folk to Reno. But I don't know what we going to do up until then."

"Why don't we go over granny's to eat?" O.D.B. suggested. He did want to see his family and hopefully run into his pop for once, being as though he haven't seen or heard from the nigga in years.

"Aight," Biz said. "Sounds good to me," and they all piled into the Cutlass.

■■■■■■

Granny, his aunts and uncles, nieces and nephews, and cousins were all more than happy to have been able to see and share Christmas dinner with Omar as they knew him, and he was equally happy. A little disappointed about the news he received about his pop and older brother, but all in all he was happy. Being around his family made him silently sing the hook to Plies' song "Family Straight" as they all left to leave:

> ♫ *My Granny On The Kidney Machine*
> *She Startin' Ta Lose All Her Weight*
> *My Auntie Got AIDS*
> *She Losing All Her Faith*
> *My Brother In Prison*
> *Second Time He Done Away*
> *My Daddy Still Smoking Dat Shit*
> *I Can See It In His Face*
> *My Lil Cousin 16*
> *Pregnant Fo A Nigga 38*
> *Before I Go, Dear Lord*
> *Let Me Get My Family Straight*

Plies: "Family Straight"

With time to kill before going to the "Rodeo Show", a popular strip club to meet Reno, they decided to cruise the city and show O.D.B. his way around. When they were younger they really didn't get a chance to do all these things because their age didn't permit them to do so. However, they were all grown now and nothing stopped them from doing anything except them.

O.D.B. looked out of the back window of his cousin's car while they rode and couldn't help but see the damage "Katrina" did even years later. By the looks of things

Kanye West was right. Bush didn't like Black people. That's why he continued to fuck the world up till the day he left the White House and went back to Texas in that helicopter. "Fuck nigga!" O.D.B. thought.

After a couple of hours of riding around the N.O. and all its sets from Holly Grove to Uptown, The Magnolia to the Calliope Projects, and the entire 9th Ward, it was time to meet the plug and O.D.B. was ready to get it over with.

Chapter Eight

Club Onyx was packed to capacity and in full swing of things when Raven and Jaquan entered just before midnight. "He was right," Raven thought about what Jaquan had told her as she observed the club. If it wasn't for the naked women walking around lap dancing and dancing naked in front of people, it would have seemed like a regular club. She had to admit, Club Onyx wasn't some trashy strip joint. It was actually nice.

Jaquan led his sister through the club proudly. Not only was he a "Boss" ass nigga, but his sister was a dime ass bitch, and the people in the club couldn't help but take notice. The two of them looked straight "Hollywood" with their furs on, but Raven is who took the spotlight when she removed her coat. The way her high heel calf high, Chanel boots hiked her ass up in her Roberta Cavali jeans with a ruffled looking beige cashmere sweater had every man in eye view of her with their eyes glued to her backside. Her ass in those jeans had her butt looking even more enticing than some of the naked broads asses did.

Raven held her pose for a few more minutes before sitting down on the chair she had tossed her coat over the back of, then the drinks started coming. Niggaz was sending her complimentary bottles of this and that. Shots of dark and white liquor with requests by the waiter but nothing worked. Raven didn't have no rap until she seen him across the bar smiling from ear to ear. She couldn't help but return the smile. He just looked so innocent.

Craig tapped his boy Anthony on the leg the moment he saw her.

"Yo check her out right there! Damn that bitch is all that!" he began.

"Man you better leave that one alone," Anthony said at the sight of the dude nearly 7' feet tall at her side. He knew him to be Jaquan, a local kingpin he went to school with.

"Why?"

"Because of that nigga next to her," Anthony told him.

"Damn! I ain't even see that nigga with her," he said defeated, and then she made eye contact with him. He smiled, and she smiled back. "Hi," he mouthed across the bar top.

"Hi," Raven said back.

Craig held his glass of Remy in the air in a gesture to offer her a drink, and she just smiled opening her arms to the bottles and glasses in front of her. Arching her eyebrows and shrugging her shoulders he knew then she had way more than enough to drink.

"Can I come join you?" he said pointing to himself then back to her.

"Yeah," she said reading his lips.

Craig stood up from his bar stool, straightened out his clothes, and then made his way over to the woman that caught his eye the minute he saw her. When he got there Jaquan gave him a cold stare, then shot his sister a look only to be told, "I'm grown!" so he left well enough alone.

"Don't worry about him. That's my brother and he's a little over-protective," Raven assured him. "Hi, I'm Raven. What's your name?"

"Craig," he responded.

For the rest of the night Craig and Raven were conjoined at the hip almost. They drank, laughed, giggled, and danced the night away as if they were the only two people in the club. For Raven it was an experience she missed dearly. For Craig, this regular Joe the Plumber type that worked at the Claymont Steele Factory, it was a once in a lifetime thing. Raven was the best Christmas present he received all day. They exchanged numbers at the end of the night and went their separate ways both thinking the same thing. "This could be the start of something good together."

■■■■■■

If you have ever been to a club in the South, you'd understand the meaning of the parking lot looked like a car show, or a bag of assorted Jolly Ranchers. There was so many candy painted cars in the car lot it didn't make no sense. It's kind of hard for me to explain it the way I want to if you haven't seen it, but if you have, well you know the rest. It was "Crunk". Biz pulled the Pepsi blue '98 Olds into the parking lot of the "Rodeo Show", the strip club Juvie talked about in that song and parked. Leading the way, O.D.B., Janelle, and Tamia all followed him up to the V.I.P. line where it cost a hundred dollars a head. And like it was nothing, Biz peeled four big face hundreds from his knot of money that seemed to be about five bands (stacks), and gave them to the bouncer at the door.

"Say Biz, what it do folk?" the bouncer talked to Biz on the first name basis.

"Aw man, ain't nuffin bruh, Just showing my kin from up North some love, that's all," Biz answered. "Showing him how to make it rain fo'real on these hoes, ya feel me?"

"Fo'sho!"

"Alright den, my nigga. See ya later bruh. Maybe at the Waffle House later on," Biz said and they headed through the door.

■■■■■■

♬ *Always Strapped*
When I Hit Da Club
Niggaz Give Me Dap
Bitches Give Me Hugs
And Since I'm Paid
Niggaz Be Muggin Me
You know I Mug 'Em Back

Lil Wayne & Birdman: "Always Strapped"

Reno sat at his reserved V.I.P. table in the back of the club that seated eight people with two of his closest homies B.G. and Juvenile. The other five seats were occupied by some groupie bitches hanging to a wing and a prayer, and the hope that one of these high profile niggaz would take them home. With his glass filled to the rim with "Yellow Rosay", his mind was occupied on the meeting of this nigga from his hometown, not bitches at his table.

"Say nigga you good?" B.G. asked his boy Reno when he noticed his odd look. "I don't need my chopper do I?"

"Naw folk, we good," Reno assured him and took a long gulp from his glass.

Tonight was the night Tommy had anticipated for a long time. The time in which he could test his new look on someone from his past to see if he'd go unnoticed, and who better than O.D.B. he thought on more than one occasion. O.D.B. was the right hand man to the little nigga Jaquan, Rasul's son, Tommy recalled. Then remembered running into them on more than one occasion. "He knows exactly who I am," Tommy thought then told himself, "if the nigga get suspicious, he going to them crocodiles down by the river in the swamp," and meant it.

■■■■■■

"Yo, where da nigga at?" O.D.B. yelled overtop of the bass that was pounding through the walls of the club.

"He's in here somewhere bruh. Relax. We going to get at da nigga folk. I told you dat nigga fuck wit me like dat bruh!" Biz said and changed a stack of his money into ones so he could throw. O.D.B. did the same thing.

Tommy Good peeped the young nigga named Biz the second he walked through the door. Soon after that, he let his eyes rest on the sight of the nigga O.D.B. and his heart began to pump a little faster. Not from fear, but from anticipation of what was about to become of their meeting. Tommy called out to one of the bouncers and had him go get Biz and O.D.B., he couldn't wait any longer.

"I told you I fuck wit da nigga like dat bruh," Biz said provingly after the bouncer left, relaying the message from Reno.

"Aight well lets go meet this nigga. I'm trying to find a new plug," O.D.B. said happily.

Tommy watched them the entire time they neared the table, and seeing O.D.B. made their last visit with one another seem like yesterday instead of the near year ago it was.

"Say Reno, this my kinfolk from up Delaware I was telling you about. O.D.B. this is Reno."

"What's good my nigga? Like a drink or some' um," Tommy asked throwing the accent on heavy.

"Yeah I'll take a sip, but say cuz, do I know you from somewhere?" O.D.B. asked. "You sure you ain't got no folk up in Delaware somewhere?" he continued, trying to put a name to the face this nigga Reno reminded him of. Then it hit him like a ton of bricks. "This nigga looks like Tommy Good!" he thought to himself, "but it can't be. I was at his funeral."

"You good my nigga?" Tommy asked staying calm. He noticed the look of confusion on O.D.B.'s face.

"Yeah I'm good," O.D.B. shook the thoughts clear from his mind, and then sat down to discuss business. An hour later O.D.B. had found his new plug. The boy Reno was going to let them go to him for eighteen thousand a piece, fifteen thousand if he brought ten kilos or better. Now say those numbers ain't sweet in a drought?! Tommy had passed the test; he was going home one day real soon.

■■■■■

O.D.B. was in such a good mood now that he had found the plug, he was all over Tamia. "Boy you a mess," she said as he whispered some bullshit like, "I want to eat your this or that," in her ear. The way his intoxicated breath tickled her earlobe when he talked sent chills up her spine. Compliments of the "E-pill" she just took, anally; yeah, in her ass. Down South they call it colon rollin' for those that don't know and you're supposed to get at least 80 percent of the pill that way as opposed to 40 to 50 percent by the mouth. Right now, Tamia was rollin' like a fool, teeth gritting and all and feelin' like a superstar. What really had her in her bag though, were the naked women throughout the club. Seeing them made her want to put the fire out between her legs, and O.D.B. was going to be the one to do it.

"Girl where'd you get them beans at?" Tamia asked Janelle, who was rollin' even harder than she was.

"From Biz. I don't know where he got 'em from, probably from Reno," Janelle answered.

"Girl what was they called again?"

"G's up—Hoes down."

"Mmm. They got my pussy drenched," Tamia told her more outgoing than normally, but that's how ecstasy pills worked. They had a way of making the shyest person come out of their shell.

"Well what you going to do about it?"

"Imma get it handled," she smiled and the DJ called out, "last call; for alcohol that is."

When the club shut down, Biz, Janelle, O.D.B., and Tamia all headed out to the Waffle House for a quick breakfast before turning in. Tamia already had it established that O.D.B. was staying with her tonight at her downtown condo, so when they pulled out, that's where Biz dropped them off at.

"Aight bruh see you tomorrow folk," Biz told O.D.B. when they were in front of Tamia's spot.

"Aight cuz," he responded.

"Tamia girl call me in the morning," Janelle said her goodbyes.

"I will," Tamia answered.

"And handle yo business," Janelle shouted from her open window.

"Say bruh," Biz called out to his cousin, "I almost forgot to tell you, you remember what granny said about them Creole girls when we were young right?"

"Nah, what?"

"Don't eat nuffin' she cooks. She might root you," he joked and smiled at Tamia.

"Boy forget you, and he ain't gotta eat none of my food. He's going to eat me! So how you like them roots?" Tamia shot back.

"I know that's right!" Janelle laughed.

"Damn bruh! It's like dat?" Biz asked O.D.B. and when he didn't answer quick enough he already knew. Tamia had her claws in his cousin. He couldn't hate though, because she was definitely wifey material. He himself had even caught himself lusting over the Creole beauty on more than one occasion, so to see his cousin with her, Biz somewhat felt he still could live out his lust because in the morning, O.D.B. was giving him every detail. Down to the way her toes looked.

"Nah cuz, it ain't nuffin' like dat," O.D.B. finally responded.

"Nigga quit flexing."

"It will be like dat," Tamia said and grabbed O.D.B. by the hand. "Come on baby, we going on in."

"Ain't dat a bitch!?" Biz laughed as Tamia pulled him away. He couldn't wait to find out what happened tomorrow.

■■■■■■

Once inside Tamia's condo, she made Omar, as she called him feel right at home. For her to be only 23 years old, from the hood, and still not a mother yet, she took pride in the way her life was going right now. She was single, had a well paying job, and didn't need a man for shit! Tamia was handling her BI (business).

"This is nice. Real nice," O.D.B. said after she gave him a tour of the place. He was now out on the balcony looking out over the city of downtown New Orleans.

"Thanks," she said modestly. "Would you like some wine?"

"What kind?"

"I got all kinds. White, red, aged. You name it, I got it."

"In that case, I'll have some white, aged wine then."

"Coming right up," Tamia said and disappeared down the hallway to the kitchen. When she returned she was carrying two glasses and a bottle of aged, Italian wine she grabbed out of the wine cellar down in the French Quarters. "One glass of aged, white wine coming right up," she said again and poured him a glass to the brim.

O.D.B. sipped the wine lightly, swishing the liquid around in his mouth before swallowing it. Something he saw on a wine tasting show. To his surprise, it really did make a difference. He could actually distinguish the grape taste from the alcohol, as the beverage eased down his throat. Tamia walked over to her entertainment system and grabbed the remote to her "Yamaha" surround system then came back to join O.D.B. on the couch.

Tamia knew Omar was watching her every move that's why she moved so smoothly around the house, always doing something with a little more seductiveness than needed. She lowered the octaves on her voice, walked with a little more twist of the hips, and loosened up on everything she was wearing when she kicked her shoes off. She unfastened the button on her Ed Hardy jeans, popped two buttons on her Oxford type shirt open to reveal her cleavage, and pulled her hair out of the bun it was in, letting it fall down to her ass. She looked stunning.

"You like it?" Tamia asked Omar about the wine when she flopped down on the corner of the couch an entire pillow away from him to pull her feet up in front of her.

"Like what? You or the wine?" he messed.

"Boy you know I'm talkin' bout the wine. You is funny," she replied and pressed the button on the remote and the soft sounds of "Destiny's Child" came through the speakers as she mouthed the words: "I'll cook your dinner, your dessert, and so much more. I want to cater to my man," then began to do everything the lyrics in the song said. When it was over, O.D.B. was back in her bedroom sprawled out on the bed with Tamia working her way up his body. The E-pill had her in full blown freak mode.

"Why you squirming and shit? Stop being a punk and take this shit," she said licking on the inside of his thighs nearing his balls ever so quickly. O.D.B. jumped again. "What? You can't take it?" she asked again as her mouth engulfed both his balls at the same time as she sucked them gently, but hard enough for them to hurt so good.

"Ssssss, damn baby that shit feels good!" O.D.B. whispered, only turning Tamia on more. She spit his balls out of her mouth, grabbed the shaft of his dick and went "Ham" on it, as she played with her pussy. For those that don't know, in the "ATL" the slang word "Ham" is short for the word mayhem, and that's just what Tamia was doing as she spit on, and slurped up her own spit from off of O.D.B.'s dick.

"Mmmm, this dick tastes good," she moaned. "Here, taste this. I taste just as good as you," Tamia said pulling her other hand from out of her pussy and putting them in his mouth. "Don't I?" she asked. Tamia was in a zone, the triple stack had her way out of character. Good thing O.D.B. knew it though, because if she would've acted this way on the "norm", he would've hit her and dismissed her as being a "freak joint" and left it like that. O.D.B. sucked her two middle fingers that were soaked with secretion and said; "Mmm-Hmm," then she pulled them out of his mouth and tasted them too. "I told you," she said and went to giving O.D.B. a boss ass head job. Tamia had the kind of head game that made you want to cut her head off and take it with you. Like now, the way her tongue and lips played around the head of his dick, then dropped down and deep throated him before coming back up and doing the same thing, had him going crazy! He couldn't take it no more so he pulled her up off him. She smiled and said with a devilish grin, "What?" She knew what the matter was.

Without saying a word, O.D.B. pulled Tamia towards him and kissed her in the mouth passionately, almost ravishly, as their tongues twisted, poked, and wrestled each other through closed mouths. Next, he let his hands roam her body softly stopping at her soft spots to give them a squeeze as they continued their tongue wrestling match. Tamia's pussy was so wet now that her juices were actually oozing out of her lips. The foreplay was almost too much to handle, so she placed her pussy on his thigh as he lay on his back and ground her hips away at his leg bringing herself to an orgasm. "Oh my God!" she let out a soft shrill, and then began to shake uncontrollably as cum ran down O.D.B.'s leg. That shit drove him crazy! O.D.B. turned Tamia over on her stomach, placed two pillows that were at the top of the bed under her pelvis to kick her ass up, and looked down at how that pussy sat right up peeking at him through her butt cheeks. He looked at it for a little while longer as Tamia rocked it back and forth for him, and then dove straight in it. Two minutes and 10 strokes later he was pulling out and jerking off on her ass. It was literally the icing on the cake.

Chapter Nine

New Years 2010 had only been in for nine hours and already was laying another one to rest. Wilmington, Delaware was becoming a warzone and really living up to the name "Hellaware" it was given by the niggaz in the street, and Jaquan was mixed up in the dead center of it. On more than one occasion he had sent his goons out to put in work that left a mother dressed in black and heartbroken, but today it was one of his own getting laid to rest, his number one gunner, "Greeny".

Jaquan had been to so many funerals in the last few years that he was numb to all the things that made a funeral sad; the sobs, the singing, the organs, the bodies, the caskets, nothing. None of those things made Jaquan feel any emotions. Taking off his hat as he entered the church, Jaquan walked up the aisle to where Greeny's casket sat. It was a closed casket funeral, but there was a huge blown up picture of him holding his son on a stand behind it. They were being buried together. Jaquan stood directly in front of the casket and stared at the picture for a moment then rubbed it before moving on. "Damn!" he thought. His heart went out to the mother and baby whose life was taken before it began.

Tamira sat at the front of the church directly in front of the casket. With tears streaming down her face, she screamed out loudly, "My baby!" and went into another hyperventilating mood as she cried. "It's okay baby. Let it out," Mom Gina said as Tamira found comfort in her bosom again. When Tamira let out yet another outburst, the entire church's heart went out to her. "My baby! Oh my God, my baby!" she cried. Just the pure agony in Tamira's voice as she cried made Brooklyn, Boochie, Keemah, and Season burst out into tears as well. The only one who wasn't buying any of her antics was Kyle. He knew the bitch, Tamira was faking and if ever there came a way for him to communicate, he was going to let it be known. Tamira peeked up from Mom Gina's breast and spotted Kiesha, and the two sorta shot each other a grin. No one had any idea.

The second outburst of "Oh my God, my baby!" made him turn around. When he did, he noticed Brooklyn, Greeny's sister and Tamira, Greeny's girl and baby mom. Sympathetically he made his way over to Brooklyn and her mother Ruthy first and gave them both hugs. Then he walked over to Tamira.

"I'm sorry about your loss," Jaquan began, "Greeny was an alright dude with me so if you happen to need anything, anything at all holla at me. Here's my business card," he told her and handed the card to her. Tamira looked at the man who she knew to be Jaquan and smiled through her tears. "Thank you," she said and knew then that it was going to be a happy fucking New Year!!!

■■■■■■

For them to only have known each other for a week, they were progressing fast. They talked on the phone while he was on break and she was in between classes, and through the wee hours of the night when they were both at home lying in their respective beds about things they both were interested in. For Raven, Craig seemed to be a blessing. He was just what she wanted in a man now that she had matured and became a mother because she was no longer into street niggaz. She couldn't see herself going through what Tommy put her through again, and she damn sure didn't want to expose her son to no negative shit.

On the flip side of things, Raven was almost like a fantasy to Craig. She was the kind of woman that nearly every man that came in contact with her tried to get. The type of woman you only see with rap stars, athletes, or drug dealers. So when she decided to give him a shot he used his honesty as an asset opposed to a negative. He told her how he was a college graduate from Del State College, a father of a beautiful little girl, divorced, and a foreman at Claymont Steele. He also told Raven of his hatred for drug dealers and the reason why. Apparently his wife had left him for a drug dealer only two years after their daughter was born. The move tore him apart mentally and spiritually, and for a few years had him in a rut. He just couldn't understand how or why she would leave when she had no needs or wants for nothing. The only logical thing he could come up with was that she wanted money now, right at that moment, and he couldn't provide it for her so she left. But life was crazy because only six months later her drug dealer boyfriend she left him for was indicted by the "Feds" for fifty kilos and sentenced to fifteen years, leaving her pregnant and unable to afford mortgage on their new house. She now relied on Section 8 to assist her in living, and the little child support she received from him.

Raven stood from the foot of her bed after strapping her heels on her feet and stood up. She walked over to her full length mirror to give herself a once over, and added her accessories to her ensemble, like her diamond tennis bracelet, watch, and necklace from Tiffany's. When she was done with her outfit, she nodded with approval as her Jimmy Choo evening gown and Chanel handbag went perfectly together. Raven looked like a black "Erica Cane". She was ready for her first date with Craig.

■■■■■■

Harry's Seafood Bar & Grille was the place of their first date. The restaurant was a new one that was located down on Wilmington's Riverfront that was now being built up like the Harbor in Baltimore, and was an ideal spot for a first date. Craig decided that the date would be here, another thing that gave him a brownie point because he took charge. Raven loved the idea of being a woman who had to follow the lead of a man because it made her feel spoiled when a man laid everything out for her. So Craig was starting off this new relationship batting one hundred. Impressive to Raven for a regular "Joe".

Craig pulled his older model Ford F-150 into Harry's parking lot and parked. He decided to get there a little early so he could be there to assist her with exiting her car and shit, a real gentleman's move on his part. He stepped out of his truck dressed to a tee and dapper as Don himself. His Sean John suit draped over him perfectly, while his full length London Fog with the scarf wrapped around his neck had him looking like a model in a newspaper ad for Boscov's.

Raven turned into the parking lot in her Beemer and spotted Craig instantly. She couldn't help but chuckle under her breath at the sight of him looking like a model in a newspaper ad, but he tried she reasoned. She drove right on by him and waved as she looked for a place to park. When she found one, she pulled down her sun visor, checked her Mac lip gloss, and feathered her hair with her fingers before preparing to get out. She reached for her handbag on the passenger seat, grabbed it and went to get out but was surprised by Craig opening her door.

"Oh," she said startled. "You scared me."

"My bad. I was only trying to be a gentleman," Craig told her holding out his hand for her to take.

"Awe you are so cute and sweet," she said. "I'm a lucky woman!" she gleamed.

"No, I'm a lucky man," he reassured her as he held her hand all the way up to the restaurant doors.

Seated at their reserved table near the back of the establishment they had a plain view of the Delaware River through a huge bay window. The sight was a subtle one as they watched a tug boat tow another boat in the direction of the Port of Wilmington, while they waited on their food. When it came, the two of them conversed through bites and sips of red wine for the entire time. After they were done they realized they enjoyed each other's company even more than they enjoyed their phone conversations.

"So, did you enjoy your meal tonight?" Craig asked Raven as they stood outside of her car.

"Yes I did Craig, but I enjoyed you more," she said honestly.

"That's nice to know."

"So, what do we do now?" Raven asked not wanting to end the night just yet.

"Come on, I have an idea," Craig told her, and the two of them walked arm in arm along the Riverfront. The stroll was romantic, and the best idea Craig could have thought of as the cold winter breeze blew in off the river causing them to cuddle even more. Raven was in la-la land in the comfortable arms of this good smelling man next to her. She looked up to the sky at all the constellations then thanked the Heavenly Father for Craig and Big Mom's advice. She was beginning to feel like herself again.

By the time they returned from their walk along the river, a whole hour had passed and the clock was nearing midnight. With both of them having to start their week off the next day, Monday, they decided to end the night off right here at Raven's car, and sealed it with a kiss. A long passionate kiss that sent juice to Raven's panties and a rock to Craig's pants. They smiled and backed away from each other when they noticed the connection, Craig's hard-on touching Raven's hip.

"We'll have plenty of time for that," she told him and slipped into the driver's seat. When she pulled off, Craig was left standing in the parking lot with a rock hard dick and blue balls. "Damn I want some of that pussy!"

■■■■■■

The nightmare seemed too real. It was as if Tommy Good really had his hand wrapped around her neck and was squeezing the life out of her. Robin sat up in bed, grabbed her throat and gasped deeply inhaling a huge amount of air to regain her normal breathing. She then got out of bed and walked to the bathroom to perform "Wudu" (Ablution for Prayer). After splashing her mouth, nose, face, head, ears, arms, and feet with cold water she went and stood on her prayer rug that faced the East. "Allah Hu Akbar!" she said raising her thumbs to the lobe of her ears then folded her arms across her chest. She needed Allah to help her fight this demon. To her Tommy Good was the devil himself. And for the life of her and all the signs Allah was sending her, she knew that he was out there somewhere lurking. "Bismil Lah Hir Rahman Nir Rahim," she started her salaat (prayer).

Chapter Ten

Jaquan got off the plane at 1:00 p.m. Eastern time in Shreveport, Louisiana with a carryon bag containing three quarters of a million dollars in cash. Today was the day he was going to meet the connect that they found courtesy of Biz, O.D.B.'s cousin. Walking through the airport towards the terminal, Jaquan noticed the stares he was receiving from a group of gentlemen in suits. His first thought was "Oh shit! The Feds!" but something about them after further analysis of them spoke something different. "Who are they?" he thought as he neared the three white men.

"Jaquan Johnson?" one of the men called out to him, stopping him in his tracks.

"Yes that's me," he responded, and the three men gleamed with excitement as they slapped fives.

"I knew that was you! Hi, my name is Jason McDonald, a scout for the N.B.A., and I want to tell you that we haven't seen a better all around two guard anywhere than you. How's the A.C.L. coming along? Are you rehabbing it? Look, here's my card. If you feel up to a workout with a team in the league give me a call," he told Jaquan and passed him a business card, then introduced him to the other scouts. "There's only one other two we seen as good as you and that was Trans "The Phantom" Owens. It's unfortunate how he turned out. Well no need to hold you up. Nice seeing you again," Jason McDonald told him and the three men walked away leaving Jaquan to ponder as he stared at their backs. He was literally offered a shot to live out his childhood dream, a chance to play in the N.B.A. "Later for that," he thought and tucked the card into his back pocket. Right now it was time to check on the flock of birds wrapped in wax paper and rubber inner tubes sealed with fabric softener to conceal the smell.

"What's up baby? You ready to do this?" O.D.B. said when Jaquan came from out of the airport.

"Been ready."

"Good. Yo this is my cousin Biz, Biz this is Jaquan."

"What's up?"

"What's good bruh? Welcome to Nawlins," Biz spoke with Southern hospitality, something Northerners were missing.

"It's my pleasure," Jaquan said.

"Nah bruh, the pleasure is all mine," Biz assured him and pulled out of the airport's terminal. In no time they were headed down a back road onto the grounds of what looked like an old slave plantation.

■■■■■

Tommy was laying on his back staring up at the T.V. monitors mounted on his bedroom walls receiving a hell of a blow job from Pat, the waitress, when he noticed the rented Charger coming down his driveway. He reached down under the covers and snatched his dick from her mouth, then rolled over to sit up on the side of his bed, leaving Pat puzzled and confused.

"Reno baby, what's da matter? You didn't like my gift to you?" she asked him.

"Nah baby, it's nuffin like dat. I'm just fittin' to take care of some real business right quick," he talked as he dressed, never taking his eyes off the monitors. For Tommy, this was the real test. His first meeting with O.D.B. had just scratched the surface. However, if he could get past Jaquan, he knew he was home free. He'd be able to go home and visit the place he missed so much, Delaware.

■■■■■■

Pulling up to the plantation that Reno called home made all three of them, Jaquan, O.D.B. and Biz feel a little uneasy. It was something about the house that seemed almost haunted in a spooky type of way. Maybe it was just from the stories that Biz was telling them about Reno and his black magic and root ways, or it could've just been the spirits of the many men and women who were raped and hung on this same plantation years ago. Whatever it was, they all agreed that they were going to handle business and get the fuck away from there as fast as they could.

Tommy met the three of them at his front door the same time they were making their way up the steps to his house. He looked to Biz and O.D.B., but really had his sight set on Jaquan. He wanted to make eye contact with him. He looked into the eyes of the lil nigga he knew as "Lil Rasul" and smiled, showing a mouthful of diamonds before extending his hand, "What's up? I'm Reno. You must be Jaquan," he said in a heavy Southern accent, and Jaquan was speechless. The man they called Reno looked exactly like Tommy Good, minus the tattoos, dreads, and diamond grill. Jaquan stared intensely. "This can't be that nigga! I was at his funeral," Jaquan said to himself, then brushed it off. "You alright folk?" Reno asked him breaking him out of his daze.

"Oh yeah, my bad cuz. You just look so familiar. You know how they say; everybody got a twin somewhere? Well you look like this nigga Tommy Good we used to know."

"Tommy Good? Oh yeah? What happened to him?" Reno asked.

"Fuck nigga got killed!" O.D.B. stated harshly.

"Damn! Dat's how y'all folk felt about dat man?"

"Hell yeah! That nigga killed my pop," Jaquan said. "All behind some broad."

"Damn baby bro, sorry to hear dat folk," Reno said, and then led them in his house. "Hold on a minute," he told them as soon as they stepped into the threshold of his house, and walked off disappearing down the hallway. When he returned, he was carrying a black crow on his shoulder where a parrot should've been. The sight was an eerie one. Another reason they wanted to get out of there. This nigga Reno was wicked.

"This way," he ordered them and they walked into a huge conference room. On the table sat 50 neatly stacked kilos with two of his armed guards on each side of the table. They each were holding AK-47s down to their sides, stone-faced and ready to kill on demand. "So who got the money?"

"I do," Jaquan said and held the carry-on bag out to him. Once Reno counted the money, almost an hour later, and Jaquan checked the work, the deal was final. Now it was time to get the work back home to Delaware, and

Jaquan had the perfect way. It just was going to take a couple days.

■■■■■■

Once the deal was finalized and Tommy had again passed the test, he was ecstatic. He was sure no one would recognize him when he returned home to the Eastside of Wilmington, Delaware. Now all he had to do was call Mike and make the arrangements. He had a whole lot of unfinished business to attend to, mainly Pretty E, Robin, and them M.O.B. niggaz lil Frankie and Fat Sal, the head of the Capelli Family. The real reason he wanted to go back was because of Raven and the son he never seen. Tommy dialed Mike's number and on the first ring he answered, "Say bro, what's up?" Mike asked.

"Nigga start up the 'Hurst', I'm coming home to pay some folk some visits," Tommy said.

"About time nigga!" Mike said, "Because I been itching to kill these folk, and the two of them hung up. What a way to start the New Year.

■■■■■■

The entire flight home, Jaquan was brainstorming on the way to get the 50 bricks home safely. Three quarters of a million dollars was way too much to chance losing at the hands of the law, so he wasn't taking any chances. Driving his rental car he left parked at the Philadelphia Airport, he drove I-95 South all the way down to 896 in Glasgow and went to his Uncle Hackett's house.

0 Pleasant Valley Road was located in the Southern most part of Delaware right before the Elkton, Maryland line. It was a little dirt road with one house and plenty of land that surrounded it. The house belonged to Jaquan's great Uncle who was strictly an outdoors man. He loved anything and everything that had to do with outside and wildlife and that's why Jaquan was paying him a visit. A visit because of the huge Pigeon Coupe he built in the back of his house where he raised them as homing birds.

"Hey there young fella! What brings you down here in these parts?" Uncle Hackett asked him before spitting out the juice from his chewing tobacco.

"Awe nuffin. Just came to check on the old fella and ask a few questions."

"About what?"

"About the pigeons."

For the next twenty minutes or so Uncle Hackett told Jaquan everything there was to know about the homing pigeons. From how fast they flew, to how far they flew. He told him that his particular breed of pigeons has won competition flights for the past two years in a row. That's all Jaquan needed to hear his mind was set. The next day Jaquan paid Uncle Hackett five thousand dollars, and had 200 of his top birds caged and shipped to New Orleans. The plan was to move half of the work this time and half the work next time because the pigeons could tote but so much. When Jaquan and the pigeons landed in New Orleans, him, O.D.B. and Biz broke the birds down in ounces. Next they put the ounces in balloons used for birthday parties and anniversaries and shit. When that was complete, they tied the balloons to the ankles of the birds then opened the cages. The birds shot straight to the sky, flew around in a complete circle as if looking for directions, then took off in the direction of the North.

Three days later, while sitting out on Uncle Hackett's back deck eyeing the Pigeon Coupe, the first bird landed. The sight of the red balloon dangling from its ankle as it sat perched on the edge of the cage made Jaquan smile from ear to ear. And for the next thirty-five minutes he watched bird after bird land home. Before he knew it, the colorful balloons made him think, and "happy birthday to me". The birds had landed literally.

Chapter Eleven

Pretty E walked into "Hood Concrete", his construction company's office bright and early this Wednesday morning, a day he usually called in, and found his new secretary, Brooke bending over looking into a file cabinet. Her ass looked like a perfectly shaped heart in her pencil skirt by Liz Claiborne, and Pretty E just had to smack it, "Smack!"

"Oh my! You scared da shit out of me!" Brooke jumped, causing papers to fly everywhere. Pretty E couldn't do nothing but laugh.

"So where is everybody?" he asked.

"Out on jobs."

"So we're here by ourselves?"

"Finally," she said.

"Lock the door," Pretty E told her, while he pulled down the blinds in the office.

Brooke locked the office door and went back to her seat behind the desk. Slowly she pulled off her panties, balled them up, and then placed them in her pocketbook, and leaned back in the chair. Pretty E's eyes were locked on her the whole time, and she knew it. Then to add some spice to the mood, she pulled both her feet up and placed them on each arm of the chair, giving him a plain view of her freshly shaven kitty. The sight instantly made his dick hard and he wanted to taste it.

"Come get it daddy," she purred then licked here lips at him. He couldn't resist. Pretty E took the bait.

■■■■■■

Brooke didn't know it would be this easy. She at least thought she'd have to put in some work to get him to fall in the trap, but all she needed to do was look nice every day. Brooke was a new employee that Tammy hired at Relax Sinsations Massage parlor. And from the moment she saw the "Help Wanted" ad in the paper for a secretary at "Hood Concrete", Tammy's plan went into effect. She sent Brooke on an interview. Just like she suspected, Brooke was hired on the spot by none other than Pretty E himself. Never in a million years would he have thought that Tammy would be behind something like this. However, a woman scorned is a woman that can't be trusted, and he was about to learn the hard way. Twenty thousand dollars was the payoff to Brooke if she could get Pretty E on tape having sex with her. So now in a bugged room with audio and visual cameras set throughout, Brooke was about to bust a twenty thousand dollar nut at the mouth of Pretty E. "Wow!" she told herself as he dove right in.

The next day for some odd reason Brooke called in and told Pretty E that she could no longer work there. He asked her did their sexcapade have anything to do with it. And she kindly told him no. What he didn't know was that right now the tape was being cut, edited, and prepared for delivery on the day of his and Egypt's wedding.

"I'm sorry baby, but you fucked with the right bitch. As long as you live I will be there to make your life miserable. So come on Eric, come home to mommy," Tammy said as she licked the envelope sealed.

■■■■■■

Ann sat at Raven's house as she got dressed to go out on her third date this week. She had become a designated babysitter for her and didn't have a problem with it. She loved tending to her nephew, Tommy Jr. Tonight though, she was in for a surprise. One she wasn't going to have any control over.

"Ok girl I'm gone. You don't need anything do you?" Raven asked heading out the door to the F-150.

"Nah girl, I'm good. I know where everything is at."

"Well he shouldn't be a problem. I just put him to sleep before you got here."

"Girl stop worrying so much and go on out there with your man," Ann said, "with his Sanford and Son truck."

"Forget you girl!" they laughed. "At least it's his."

"Bye."

"Bye. I'll see you later on."

"Take your time. Enjoy yourself."

"I will. Thanks Ann."

"Girl that's what I'm here for," she said, and Raven walked out the door.

After watching a movie on "On Demand" and checking on the baby, Ann decided to whip up a little something to eat for herself. She walked in the kitchen, looked through the cabinets and refrigerator, and decided on some minute steaks and tater tots. When she was done and heading back into the living room with her plate to watch another movie, in he walked through the front door. Surprise!

■■■■■■

Wednesday night, hump night, and not a single thing to do in the city, Jaquan rode around aimlessly trying to find something to get into. He rode through the Westside, the Eastside, South Bridge, Riverside, the North side, Market St., and Cash Ave., but still there was nothing. "Where is everybody at?" he asked himself, but remembered the police had it so hot from all the recent shootings that the streets were almost empty. Finally, giving up and deciding to call it a night, Jaquan decided to go see his sister and nephew before driving home to Greenville. He knew she was there because her car was parked in the driveway. He dug down into his pocket for his house keys and looked through the ring for Raven's. When he found it, he walked right in. Surprise!

■■■■■■

"Raven," he called out when he entered the house. "Where you at girl?"

"Boy, be quiet yelling like that before you wake that baby up," Ann said smiling.

"Oh shit, what's good? Where my sister at?"

"She went out on another date with Craig."

"Damn! Again?"

"Mmm-hmm. They real hot and heavy right now."

"Dat's what's up."

"So what's up wit 'chu? What 'chu doing tonight?" Ann asked.

"Nuffin. I was about to go home."

"Well I know I'm a get my hug first right?"

"And you know it," he said and hugged her extra tightly.

Ann snuggled into Jaquan's embrace, burying her face into his chest. His arms felt soothing around her body like it was where she was supposed to be, and it made her feel uneasy. She began to question her love for Mike, but quickly shook that thought from her head. "It's just a foolish lust," she told herself, realizing she hadn't been with no one else besides Mike. And that reason alone had her wondering. She squoze him back. Before she knew what was happening she got caught in the moment and ravishly kissed Jaquan in the mouth.

When their lips locked, Jaquan thought, "I got her now," he knew she was married to Mike Cottman, but "Fuck that!" he was about to be one up on the nigga who was the best friend of the man who killed his father, Tommy Good. And what better way to get back then by fuckin that nigga'z wife. So as their kiss became more intense, he began to tear at her clothes. When she didn't stop him and began to tear at his clothes also, he picked her up and carried her over to the couch and laid her down. Standing over top of Ann as she laid naked on the couch, Jaquan looked on in admiration. He smiled. Ann smiled too. The next thing she remembered was giving into temptation, and falling weak to her lust as one leg rested on his should and the other wrapped around his waist as Jaquan stroked away. When it was all said and done with, Ann thought, "What have I done?" While Jaquan thought, "I'm one up on that nigga!" For them, it was a moment they'd both take to their graves.

Chapter Twelve

Mike sat at the American Airlines departure exit at the Philadelphia International Airport and waited for him to walk out. It had been just a little over a year since he last saw him and he was just as excited as Tommy was about his return than Tommy was himself. On more times than none, Mike tried to imagine what Tommy looked like these days, especially after Tommy would describe himself over the phone and text pictures that never came through clearly. However, he could never get a clear vision of him in his mind. So as he sat in the "Hurst", the black on black Celebrity with the limo tint, listening to "Hail Mary" by Tupac and mouthing the words. "God said he would give his only begotten son to lead the wild in the ways of the land. Follow me!!" he waited for the return of the man Tommy Good. "I ain't a killer but don't push me/Revenge is like the sweetest joy next to getting pussy," Mike sang as the bass pounded and his adrenaline pumped. The City of Wilmington was in for a storm the weather man hadn't forecasted.

Tommy stepped off of the plane and was greeted by something he didn't know he could miss, the cold winter air of the North. He tucked his chin from the wind that was blowing a misty snow and moved through the people swiftly as they entered the airport. "Damn it's cold out this muthafucka!" he thought as he headed to the exit without a piece of luggage. When he walked out to the departure deck, the first thing he spotted was the "Hurst", and a smile he hadn't smiled in a long time crossed his face. Tommy grabbed the handle to the passenger side door and snatched it open.

"Say bro what's da deal my nigga?" Tommy asked Mike with a smile as his dreads hung, nearly hiding his face.

"What's happening folk?" Mike answered in his own Southern drawl.

"Man I'm just happy to be back from the dead," he told him with a sinister smile. "Now it's time to handle some business."

"Who first?" Mike asked not really caring one way or the other. He was just happy to be back putting in work.

"The nigga Fat Sal." Let's send a message to Lil Frank that he picked the wrong nigga to fuck wit," Tommy answered, and then asked, "How's Raven?"

"I'll let you find that out by yo' self. She good though."

"What's dat supposed to mean?"

"Let's just say you're back in time, because she was about to move on."

"Move on?"

"Yeah, wit some regular "Joe" nigga."

"Oh no, I ain't having dat shit."

"I knew you wouldn't," Mike said with a laugh, and pulled off heading South on I-95 towards Delaware.

Tommy tilted his seat back, let his head rest on the headrest, and stared out of the windshield of the "Hurst" at all the familiar sights he had missed over the past year and some change. It was nothing like the sights of New Orleans, The Super Dome, historical downtown, and the French Quarters were tourist attractions, but it was also home. And just to see the sign that read: "Welcome to Delaware — A Place to Be Somebody" had him glad to be back. There were so many things he wanted to do, and so many people he wanted to see that he didn't think he'd have enough time to do it all in the couple days he was back. There were two people that were mandatory for him to see on his list and that was Big Mom and Raven. He wanted to see Ann too, and had no idea that was about to happen.

"Yo Mike, drop me off at Raven's," he told him and Mike headed to the house in Pike Creek. Had they got there five minutes earlier, Mike would have gotten the surprise of a lifetime. One that would have took the lives of both Ann and Jaquan.

■■■■■■

Pulling up to the house brought back memories of Tommy's that he thought he forgot. The fondest being Joey "Gunz" posed as a mailman. Then there was the day he first brought it at three hundred thousand for his grandmother who turned it down. Now he was about to create some new memories, ones of him reuniting with Raven, and meeting his son for the first time. Mike parked the car.

Ann heard the car doors shutting and thought, "Damn she home early," before going to peek out the window. When she did, her heart dropped the minute she saw her husband and a man she never seen before. Mainly because she was still half naked, half naked because she was still basking in the donkey dicking she received just minutes ago. "Shit!" she exclaimed then ran back to the living room to snatch up her clothes and got dressed in the bathroom. Then she heard the front door open. "How da fuck do he got keys to this house?" a question that would be answered soon enough.

At the door, Tommy pulled his keys from his pocket and tried them just because. To his surprise the locks were still the same. Stepping into the house was like stepping back into time because the house was identical to the way he left it, except for the portraits and new "knick-knacks" Raven had used to add her own personal touch. The furniture, the lamps, the end tables, and all that was the same, so he figured she left it that way to hold onto a piece of him after his death in which he was right. That was Raven's sole purpose of keeping everything.

Ann came out of the bathroom the minute she was dressed and heard Mike and the unidentified man talking. She walked towards the sound of the voices and said, "Mike, what are you doing here?"

"Oh shit babe. I didn't know you were here," Mike replied.

"And who is this that you are bringing into this girl's house? and how'd you get keys?" she asked as the man still had his back turned to her looking at all the pictures on the walls, tables, and over top of the mantelpiece. When Tommy turned around towards Ann and smiled, she lost it!!

"What's up Annie-Fannie!?" he teased her with the nickname he gave her as a child, and she burst out into tears and screams of joy. She couldn't believe it. There was no way in the world that this man standing before her with a head full of dreads, a mouthful of diamonds, and a face full of tattoo tears was Tommy Good. She was at his funeral. But it was, he was alive and standing right before her in the flesh. She shot past her husband Mike trying to get to Tommy so fast she almost knocked him down.

"Oh my God! Tommy it's you!" she cried happily, then smacked the shit out of his arm. "Boy don't ever scare me like that again! We thought you were dead!" Ann said.

"I am," Tommy said with a wink and a smile. "Ann we need to let people keep thinking that, you dig?"

"Ok," she said still holding on to him tight.

"You can let me go now, I ain't going nowhere," he said. "I promise."

■■■■■■

Raven and Craig pulled up to her house a little past eleven o' clock that evening. Seeing the light from the television flicker through one of the windows, she assumed Ann was probably watching a movie like she always did. But Raven had plans of her own tonight. Tonight she was giving Craig some pussy, something that she had been contemplating since the first date they had together. And although it took plenty of thought, and even more nerve, she was ready. The fire between her legs needed to be extinguished, and her dildo was no longer footing the bill.

"Do you want to come inside?" she asked him, catching him by surprise.

"Are you sure you would like me to?" he asked seriously. Because he knew of Raven's past and all of the things she'd been through, and in no way did he want her making premature judgments that may cause turmoil later on.

"Yes I'm sure," she told him and he parked. "I take you parking as a yes, right?"

"Of course I'm coming," he grinned as they made eye contact, and right then, the moment their eyes locked, they knew that tonight was the night, the night they consummated their relationship by having sex, a night that seemed to be long overdue.

■■■■■

After talking to Ann and Mike, and familiarizing himself with everything that was happening in the city, he sent them home. He wanted to be there by himself when Raven came home from her date because he knew it was going to be an emotional reunion. Part of him was angry that she had decided to move on, and part of him wanted to react like he always did and eliminate the problem, but all in all for the most part he was happy for her either way it went. She deserved to be happy. And after contemplating on it for a little while longer, he couldn't find one reason why she shouldn't have moved on with her life. He was dead for Christ sake. It wouldn't have made no sense in the world for her to hold on to possibilities that a dead man would return. That was unheard of. The only people who believed in reincarnation of the human flesh were the people who believed in voodoo, black magic, and witchcraft. The thing that was crazy about it all though, was that it does exist. This is no

Harry Potter shit, this is real. It's a satanic art that has been practiced for years and years in Africa, Haiti, Jamaica, and other foreign countries, as well as in the South. If you don't believe me read your Bible or the Quran, and it will clearly warn you to stay away from the things I mentioned. Better yet, talk to someone who has been affected by roots. See if they'll tell you that it's fake. So for Raven to have moved on was expected from Tommy's view. The question was just, what was she going to do now that he was back?

Outside of Raven's front door, she hesitated before turning to Craig, "Hold on a minute. Let me make sure Ann is decent before I invite you in," she told him and went inside. She called her name, but Ann didn't answer. She figured she was asleep. Raven walked into the living room to see if her guess was right and there in the dark sat some man holding her baby. "Craig!!" she screamed at the top of her lungs, causing him to come bursting into the house and running to the sound of her voice.

"What's the matter?" he said coming to her rescue.

"Look," she pointed to the man.

Tommy was surprised by the way Raven screamed at the top of her lungs like that. Her voice had awakened the baby and Tommy Jr. cried out at the top of his little heart. He was about to hop up, hit the light, and tell her who he was, but he decided to let it play out. He wanted to see where he stood. Raven turned on the light switch lighting the entire living room up and got a closer look at the man holding her son and wiped her eyes clear. They had to be seeing things. But when the man spoke, and said, "So this is my junior, huh boo?" she fainted and fell back into Craig's arms. He was just as shocked as she was when the man said his junior. Right then Craig knew that any hopes of him getting some pussy tonight was shot down and went straight out the window.

"I'll take over from here money," Tommy told Craig and took Raven from out of his arms and laid her down on the couch. After that Tommy turned to Craig and explained as much as he could without going into detail. He let him know that it would be best for him to get in his F-150 and take his ass home before it "be's" something, lifting his shirt, revealing the chrome .357 magnum on his waist line. At the sight of the gun, Craig knew what Tommy was saying was right. So after having Tommy agree to have Raven call him, he left.

"Pussy!" Tommy thought.

■■■■■■

When Raven finally came to and regained some focus in her eyes after batting them repeatedly, they focused in on the man sitting at her side. His face was familiar to her, but the dreads and tattoos changed him to a certain degree. You really had to look past all that to see that this man was actually Tommy Good, and when Raven realized it, tears began to stain her cheeks. This was all a bad dream, a nightmare to her. "Why was God playing tricks on her?" she asked.

"Raven baby, are you ok?" Tommy spoke. It wasn't a dream he was really here right in front of her eyes.

"How? I, I, I," she stuttered. "I thought you were, were, were…"

"Dead?" he helped her out.

"Yes. How? Why? What happened to you? Where you been?" Raven asked question after question.

Tommy inhaled deep, let out a long sigh, and then began with the answers. He didn't know where to start, but he managed, telling Raven everything he could about the past year leaving out nothing except the voodoo. He even told her he was her crank caller, the one who was playing on her phone all those times. That made her smile, but deep down inside she was still mad. The question that still seemed unanswered to her, and she had no logic to, was the reason he just left her and his son behind like that. Was his freedom more important than his family? Were a few punk ass years in jail for faking his death worth all this? Those were the questions that meant the most to Raven, and those were the questions he just couldn't seem to answer. Yes, she was glad he came back and was alive and well, but was he worth the risk and chance of her going through the same things twice? How'd she know she wouldn't have to bury him again? All these were questions she asked herself about Tommy. Then there was Craig, her baby. She had a hell of a choice to make and fast; the choice of going with her heart and mind? Or going with love? In the end, her heart would win. Craig would be her ultimate decision, and she would be glad that she made that choice because lightning does strike twice.

Chapter Thirteen

Six months after coming out of the full body cast and going through hours of therapy, Lil Frank Marachi III still walked with a limp thanks to that old box Chevy Caprice that ran him over that night. Lil Frankie walked to the window of his condo and stared out at the city, his city. The new Capelli Family had managed to take back power over the Port of Wilmington and had all the small businesses paying a luxury tax to them. It was the La Costra Nostra way. Give the companies an option. Pay taxes or continue to get robbed and stolen from until it bankrupted you. So the small business owners agreed. It was better to join them than go against them. At least that's what a wise man would do because in the end you still had your business.

"Baby do you want your eggs scrambled or fried?" his fiancée Kia called from the kitchen.

"Fried," he yelled back and minutes later Kia came out to the living room carrying their son, Lil Frank IV in her arms and a plate in her hands. "Thanks baby."

"Mmm-hmm," she said and turned to leave.

Lil Frankie couldn't be happier than he was now about the way his life was going as he watched his soon to be wife walk away. Everything was falling right in place for him. There was only one thing that bothered him on a daily basis, and that was the fact that he couldn't get the moolie Tommy Good before anyone else did. He knew he was responsible for him getting hit by that car, and since Tommy was no longer around, the only thing left to do was get the driver, Mike Cottman.

The same time Lil Frankie was plotting his next move in his condo that overlooked the city; Mike and Tommy were putting theirs in effect. Fat Sal was going to be their first victim. They figured they'd hit the power first because it would send out more of a statement. Anytime something happened to the M.O.B., it sent out a message and a fear in the heart of others. So they knew this killing had to be high profile for all to see, and they had the perfect way to do it.

Tommy and Mike sat outside of the Italian Sub shop, Capriotti's on Union St. waiting for Fat Sal to come out. It was only five o' clock in the evening but already the sun had gone down. It was like that in the winter months on the East Coast. It always got dark early due to the time going up. They had followed him here from Little Italy's Bar & Lounge right around the corner, and were glad to see he was alone. It would be less of a problem this way they knew so they masked up.

Being as though it snowed last night, Fat Sal tiptoed on the sidewalk when he came out of the sub shop. In one hand he carried his pineapple soda, and in the other hand he carried his extra large Italian sub with extra meat. As he slowly approached his car, the only thing that was on his mind was the sub in his bag that had the oil seeping through the outer wrapper. His mouth watered at the thought of all the pickles and hot peppers that were about to fill his mouth so he never noticed the two masked men approach him from behind. As soon as he placed his key in the driver side door of his Lincoln Navigator, he felt the cold steel pressed up on the side of his fat neck that was cherry red from the cold.

"Don't make a scene nigga. Just slide ya fat ass across those seats," Mike spoke through clenched teeth with attitude.

"Hey, what's going on?" Fat Sal asked.

"Just do as you're told," Mike instructed him, then turned to Tommy. "What Sha-Rock used to say?"

"Caught 'em slippin'," Tommy laughed and kicked Fat Sal up his ass. "Hurry up nigga!"

"I'm a follow behind you in the "Hurst"," Mike said before going on. "And keep dat fat mufucka at gun point! If he moves an inch, shoot his fat ass."

"You know I got it," Tommy told him and pulled away from the sidewalk of 8th and Lincoln St. headed to I-95 North. They had something in store for Fat Sal's ass so Tommy took off his mask. He looked to Fat Sal and said, "Eat your last meal."

Fat Sal couldn't believe his eyes. It was Tommy Good. He knew then that indeed this was his last meal. He took the biggest bite he could, chewed it up, and farted at the same time from nervousness.

■■■■■

The next morning, three bus loads of school kids on a field trip to the Philadelphia Zoo, were greeted by the grotesque sight of the Polar Bear cage with the pool surrounding it. There for all to see was the gruesome discovery of Fat Sal's body torn apart by the huge two-thousand pound bears. His legs and arms floated in the bloody red pool with one hand still clutching what appeared to be a half of a sub. His torso and head were still connected, and lying up near the opening of the cage next to two bloody red polar bears from the snout to the feet. Sub wrappers were everywhere. The kids all screamed and ran away crying. Ten minutes later, news vans were everywhere.

■■■■■■

Lil Frankie hadn't heard from Fat Sal all night long last night and was beginning to worry about his best friend and under boss. He called his cell phone and left message after message until finally deciding to call Gloria, Fat Sal's fiancée. When she told him she hadn't heard from him either, he knew something was wrong. That's why he headed over to Lil Italy's Bar & Lounge. That's the last place Fat Sal was yesterday, and he was sure one of the fellas knew his whereabouts.

Once inside of Lil Italy's Lil Frankie was greeted with respect (firm handshakes and kisses on the cheeks). His family of a new wave of Capelli members was all sitting around watching the six o' clock news with Jim O'Brien and Monica Malpass, as they sipped beers and downed shots of Rum and Vodka.

"Hey boss! You gotta see this!" one of the Capos called out to Lil Frankie and pointed to the T.V. "This have to be the most hilarious shit I ever seen!" he finished.

"Yeah boss. "Knucks" is right. This shit is hilarious!" a newly made man named Carmine Figarelo added as they all became silent to watch the repeat of the breaking news.

"Good evening everyone. I'm Rick Edwards, and I'm Monica Malpass, and this is the six o' clock news," they began.

"In breaking news tonight, we're going to go in live with Chopper Six and Lauren Wilson on the scene of a tragic school field trip for a group of elementary students this morning at the Philadelphia Zoo. I'm Monica Malpass what do we have Lauren?"

"Good evening Monica and hello everyone. I'm Lauren Wilson, and I'm here live at the Philadelphia Zoo on Grad Ave. where today zookeepers, who were supposed to feed the polar bears', were greeted by a huge surprise. Apparently a man had snuck into the zoo drunk and fell into the polar bears' den eating a large Italian hoagie that triggered the bears into frenzy. By the time anyone got here this morning, the man had been torn apart and partially eaten. As of now there is no foul play suspected!" she talked loudly over the helicopter's propellers. "We'll have more at eleven o' clock."

"Thank you Lauren. And in sports," Rick Edwards began, "the fighting Phillies just acquired Ichizo Zuzuki in a three team trade from the Seattle Mariners," he began the sports section of the news.

"Did ya hear dat boss?! A fucking large sub!" Carmine continued on, ignoring the rest of the news, but Lil Frankie was still laughing.

"I have to admit that was some funny shit!" Lil Frankie said, and then asked, "Has anyone seen Fat Sal today?"

"No. The last time I saw him was yesterday this time," "Knucks" answered. He earned the name "Knucks", which was short for "Knuckles" because his hands were the size of Andre the Giants and he was only 5'7".

"Where'd he say he was going?"

"Around Union St. to Capriotti's," he told him and Lil Frankie was out the door. When the owner of the sub shop said they seen Fat Sal and a black guy leave in his truck together followed by a black, old model Celebrity, he already knew what it was. Mike Cottman was back at it. "If it's war that fucking moolie wants, its war he gets!" Lil Frankie told himself, and then his phone rang. "Yeah" he answered.

"Oh my God Frankie it was Sal, my beautiful Salvatore!" Gloria, his fiancée cried into the phone.

"Gloria what are you talking about?"

"On the news in the polar bear cage, they found his wallet at the bottom of the pool," then it all added up. Lil Frankie was devastated with the news of his friend, but he did manage a smile through all the pain. And although the men in that black Celebrity took his life, they didn't take his sub. "Not even the polar bear," he thought about the hand that still clutched the half of a sub. "Sal you fat fuck!" Lil Frankie said to himself and laughed and cried at the same time.

"Don't worry Gloria. I'll get to the bottom of this," he told her and hung up the phone. "Mike Cottman and this mystery man were dead men," Lil Frankie promised himself.

■■■■■■

Killing just did something to Mike. It was like the sun on a stormy day; like your team winning the Super

Bowl; like busting a long overdue nut in the woman of your dreams; and like hitting the lottery. It just made him feel normal and at ease. No tension at all. Just the need to relieve the hard-on that killing gave him at just the thought. Like now, he couldn't wait to put his sons on the school bus and get back in the house with Ann, who was his teacher for the day in yet another role playing event. His mind was so preoccupied with the thought of his wife Ann that he never noticed the Lincoln Town car and black Maserati parked down the street.

■■■■■■

The minute Lil Frankie saw Mike come out of the house; he notified his hit squad in the Lincoln that the man who just walked out of the house was indeed the man they wanted.

"That's him, but like I said, no women and kids. They're innocent in all of this. This is about the men," Lil Frankie told the leader of his hit squad, "Knucks".

"Ok boss. Just give us the go," he responded.

■■■■■■

When Mike got back into the house, he went to the kitchen to grab an apple. The next thing he did was grabbed his son's last year book bag out the hallway closet and threw it over his shoulder. He was going to school.

■■■■■■

Ann was downstairs in the basement sitting on the pool table she had decorated like her classroom desk. In front of the pool table, she had a chair and snack tray set up in front of it like a student's desk, and on top was everything from rulers to crayons. The only thing missing was her student.

"You're late for homeroom Michael!" she yelled upstairs. "Do you want detention? No, better yet, how about the paddle. Do you want that?"

"No Mrs. Cottman! I'm coming right away ok?" he said like a bashful kid.

"Well you better hurry up because it's role call," she announced and he appeared down the basement steps.

"This is for you Mrs. Cottman," Mike said when he handed her the apple, and they both fell out laughing. They just couldn't hold it in any longer.

"Boy you are crazy!" Ann chuckled.

"Not as crazy as you," he said and again they made love like the very first time. "Mrs. Cottman, is this extra credit?" Mike asked as they lay across the pool table.

"No honey. That was a pop quiz. This is extra credit," Ann said and took her husband's manhood into her mouth. Feeling guilty about her episode with Jaquan, Ann tried to suck the blood out of him. When they were done they were sweaty and exhausted. Ann jumped up and ran to the shower, and Mike just laid there. If only he knew what was about to happen.

■■■■■■

Lil Frankie watched as his five man hit squad made their way onto the lawn of Mike's house and up to his door. Lenny "The Lock" as he was known led the way. He earned the name "The Lock" because he specialized in burglaries. There wasn't a lock or device that could stop him from getting into anywhere he wanted. Like now, within a few seconds he had the door open and they were going in. Lil Frankie pulled off with a smile. "Fucking moolie! Meet your maker," he said to himself as he drove down the street and out of the development.

The Capelli Family Hit Squad moved throughout Mike and Ann's house as stealthy as a bomber used in the military. Mike didn't hear a thing. In fact, he was dozed off in a light sleep until he felt the rope wrapped around his neck and the smack of a huge hand across his face.

"Wake the fuck up! You fucking piece of shit!" Knucks, the one who smacked him said, while Lenny "The Lock" held the rope around his neck tightly, nearly strangling him.

"Man fuck you pussy!" Mike spat totally disregarding the five men who was standing before him with aluminum bats. He fought and struggled like hell to get away, and then they took batting practice on his body as Mike hollered from the pain. Each swing of the bat felt as if it was breaking a bone on his body, but he never stopped fighting. "Do what you going to do pussies! Kill me! You faggot mufuckas," Mike cursed between yells and Ann heard the last statement.

"Kill me?" she thought as she stepped out of the shower.

Ann listened even more intensely as she slipped on her robe. She didn't bother with drying off because she was too worried about what she just heard, and the well-being of her husband. The way Mike was hollering had scared her to death and she knew something was wrong.

Mike had always prepared her for a day like this in the event that something like this ever happened, but she didn't think it ever would. Her heart was racing like never before and the screams Mike was letting out brought tears to her eyes. "I'm coming baby!" Ann spoke to herself as if Mike could hear her and she lifted up their mattress to grab it. There it was, the AK-47 that he had taught her to shoot. She picked it up, tucked it under her shoulder and tied her robe back up. She was on her way to the basement.

Ann stuck her head in the basement door and peeked down into the basement. What she saw filled her heart with a rage she didn't know she could possess as she saw the way they were beating her husband. Mike's face was covered with blood and his body was limp as if he was dead and Ann cried out, "Get the fuck away from my husband!" and pulled out the AK-47. In a blind rage she blanked out and held her finger on the modified trigger. When the last bullet, the 57th one was fired from the clip, there in the middle of her basement floor laid five dead men and one wounded her husband. She had accidentally shot him too. The good thing though, was that she only grazed him.

Mike heard Ann scream, "Get away from my husband!" then the barrage of bullets that came flying from the top of the steps as she walked down them. Mike tried to roll up under the pool table to get out of harm's way because Ann wasn't aiming; she was just shooting with bad intensions. But he couldn't get out of the way fast enough. One of the bullets tore through the flesh of his thigh, but he'd live. It went in and out cleanly.

"Baby, baby! Are you alright?" Ann said dropping the gun and running to her husband's aide.

"Yeah baby, I'm good. Come help me get out of here though. I'm shot," Mike said.

"Ok, but baby we gotta clean up," she said.

"Nah baby, just torch the place," Mike told her, and she helped him up the stairs and out to the car.

For the next fifteen minutes, Mike sat in the family R500 Benz waiting patiently as Ann brought all their jewelry and money they had stashed away in the house for a rainy day. He smiled like a muthafucka the more he thought about what just happened, and how his wife handled her business. Years and years of being with him turned her into a killer just like him. The house went up in flames, and Ann backed out the driveway. They had already planned out their next move. Pick the kids up, head up to the cabin in the Poconos, and call Marcus, Tommy's brother, for the fake passports. It was time to leave the country.

"How you feel baby?" Mike asked her as she drove away from their home.

"Like a mufucking killer!" she smiled and looked through the mirror of the car at the smoke she left behind. "What are you going to do about that baby?" she asked Mike about the bullet hole.

"Imma let that shit drip dry," he smiled. "I'm a soldier baby."

"And I'll go to war with you any day," she said and kissed him at the red light.

■■■■■

Lil Frankie had driven straight back to Lil Italy's Bar & Lounge when his men entered the house. He didn't want to be seen by any eyewitnesses at all, and he definitely didn't want to be I.D.'d as being anywhere near the scene of the crime when it all went down, so now as he sat in his office with his feet up on the desk talking to Jaquan on the phone and watching the twelve o' clock news, he waited for his squad to return. He told Jaquan about the events with Fat Sal and how he just handled Mike in so many words. Told him how the owner gave him the drop on a black Celebrity and the two men who were in it. Then he told him how he figured it was Mike Cottman. The only question he had remaining was, who was the other guy? That's when Jaquan put two and two together.

"What he look like?"

"The owner said he had some kind of glittery teeth and dreadlocks, like a Jamaican."

"Dreadlocks?" Jaquan asked himself more so than Lil Frankie. "And a glittery grill?"

"Yeah he also had tattoos on his face," and that's what did it. Jaquan knew exactly who he was. The unknown man was Tommy Good.

"It was Tommy Good."

"Tommy Good?"

"Yeah I seen him in New Orleans," Jaquan said. He had to warn his uncle, Pretty E and notify Raven and Robin too. He had a whole lot of ground to cover in a little bit of time.

"Well what are we going to do?"

"Let me call you back," Jaquan said and Lil Frankie turned his attention to the T.V. screen. His heart dropped when he saw the firemen bring out five body bags. "Shit!"

Chapter Fourteen

The killings that took place at Mike's house a week ago had everyone talking and the police on the lookout. Mike wasn't a suspect the police led everyone to believe, but we know how that goes. Turn yourself in and be charged with "Murder One". The biggest talk though, was the talk about Tommy Good being alive. People couldn't believe their ears or eyes until a news flash appeared on the screen and a picture captured by a camera on Union St. ran by Downtown Visions of Wilmington showed a close up of him and Mike putting pistols to Fat Sal's neck as he neared his Navigator.

The freeze framed photo was unmistakable. It was Tommy Good, and police were combing the areas asking everyone the whereabouts of these two men.

Craig called Raven the moment he saw the latest on the news. She had been an emotional wreck from the night he took her home and Tommy was sitting in the living room, and he had been doing his best to be there for her. He was also counting his blessings after seeing what Tommy and Mike were capable of because he remembered the size of the gun on Tommy's waist line that he flashed on him before telling him to get in his F150 and leave.

"Are you sure you're ok?" Craig asked her as she sorta just stayed silent on the other end of the phone.

"Yes I'm sure baby. It's just so much right now. Can you imagine burying the love of your life only to have them return a year and a half later?"

"I can't say I can."

"That's what I know. Nobody can, but I'm dealing with it right now. Craig baby, that's why I've been distant from you since that night at my house, I needed some time to think. Think about Tommy, think about us. My love, the love I have for Tommy was telling me to go with him. However, my heart and my mind were telling me to stay with you, so I had a decision to make. And I must tell you it wasn't easy. I did however make my decision. And I'm glad I decided like I did. I chose you Craig. You are who I choose to be with, and just think I really contemplated the thought of being with Tommy. I would've been a fugitive too. Poor Ann, I feel for her," Raven said as Ann's photo crossed the television screen too.

"And I'm glad you did ma," Craig said happily. "I don't know if I ever told you this, but baby you are my dream girl. It is unbelievable that a woman like you would even consider a man like me. I'm a regular "Joe Blow" type of guy," he said to her again, and she blushed on the other side of the phone because she knew then that she was going to be more than loved. She was going to be respected and appreciated.

"Craig baby, I don't know what I would do without you," Raven said. "Where are you at?"

"I'm home."

"Would you mind keeping me company?"

"It would be my pleasure," he said.

Tonight was going to be the night that the two of them, Raven and Craig, would explore each other's calling a little deeper. They were going to make love for the first time.

■■■■■

Tommy, Mike, Ann, and the kids were all up the Poconos in the mountains at the cabin Marcus owned. They had been there for almost a month now in hiding, letting the heat of the police die down, and Mike heal up from the beating he received at the hands of the Capellis. In their possession they held their own individual, fake passports, courtesy of Marcus and his partner Dave, the white boy who Tommy first met up here with Raven. They had it all mapped out. Finish the job they started by taking out Pretty E, Lil Frankie, and Robin, and then flee the country. Go to South America with Fidel Castro's people and Assata Shakur, a place where the United States couldn't touch you. Tommy walked out of the cabin into the snow filled night air and decided to call a person of his past. One who he was sure would keep him posted on what was going on in the City of Wilmington.

"Relax Sinsations," the sultry voice of Tammy answered.

"What's up baby? How you been?" Tommy asked her.

"Who's this?"

"It's me, Tommy. Tommy Good," he said and Tammy smiled.

"Mr. Goodbar! How have you been? And what have you gotten yourself into this time? You have been all over the news. They even had you and Mike on America's Most Wanted. John Walsh painted y'all out to be the worst people alive. They even had your house in New Orleans on there. Boy you is crazy. Them people pulled tarot cards, crystal balls, and all kinds of shit out of your house. Said you was heavy into roots and shit," Tammy rambled. "Is that true?"

"Yeah I believe in roots. Why?"

"Ain't no particular reason. Shit, whatever floats your boat. If you like it, I love it."

"I know that's right. So what's been going on in Delaware? I need you to keep me posted ok, especially about that nigga Pretty E. That nigga tried to kill me," he said and that was music to Tammy's ears.

"You know I gotchu. But how am I supposed to keep in touch with you?"

"I'll keep in touch with you."

"Ok Mr. Goodbar."

"Ok ma," he said and they hung up the phone.

Tommy knew that after that call, Pretty E was just a phone call from his top off. Ain't it funny how life worked?

Chapter Fifteen

The rest of the winter went by without another incident from Tommy Good and Mike Cottman. The people and law enforcement agencies had figured that the "America's Most Wanted" airing had them so far in hiding that they'd never come back out into public. It was already assumed that they were out of the country somewhere sipping Mai Tais, so everyone sorta just went on with their normal lives. Tommy Good and Mike Cottman were a thing of the past. Today, though, was the first day of spring, and the day of the wedding. The wedding vows were about to be exchanged by Pretty E and Egypt. The church was packed and God had made the weather a perfect 75 degrees, sunny and mild. Today was going to be a special one Pretty E knew. He just wished his brothers Hit Man, Dog, and Rasul were there to see it. They probably was turning over in their graves laughing like a mufucka at Pretty E in his "Tux" about to be married, and the thought made him smile. "Fuck you niggaz," he said to himself.

Inside the church in a separate room away from where the actual ceremony was about to take place, Egypt was getting made-up, dressed, and crowned with her head piece. This was the day she had waited for all her life. The day she dreamed of as a little girl, the day some man would make her his bride. Sitting in the chair in front of the huge mirror while the make-up artist and hair dresser did her hair, she remembered the days on the green box in the projects that she and Pretty E used to plan out this day together. It was almost unbelievable that all these many years, and a son later they were actually about to do it, take the leap, and she was all smiles and tears.

"Awe baby, what's da matter?" the make-up artist asked her as her newly lined make-up ran down her cheeks. "Don't cry baby. This is your day! You're supposed to be happy."

"I am. That's why I'm crying," she told her as every woman in the room tried to console her.

"Now baby come on. It's going to be fine," Egypt's mother assured her child with a strong hug and kiss on the cheek.

"Ok mommy."

"Now let's get it together ok? You have a wedding to go to. Your husband to be is going to be waiting."

"Ok mommy," she repeated, and then there was a knock on the door.

"Who is it?" her best friend Tish asked. They grew up in Riverside together, her, Tish, Tasheena, and Rayon.

"FedEx, I have a package for a Ms. Egypt Wright," the man on the other side of the door said.

"A package," Egypt asked herself. "Who would be sending a package?" Then she thought, "Probably Eric trying to be romantic."

Tish walked over to the door and opened it, letting the man in the FedEx uniform in. He walked over to the woman that everyone told him was Egypt and had her sign the clipboard before handing him the manila envelope.

"Thank you," she said and tore it open.

"What is it girl?" Rayon asked.

"I know let me see," Tasheena said.

"Damn! Wait a minute, can I see it first?!" Egypt said clutching the envelope to her chest, and backing them up. Once they were at bay, Egypt slowly opened the envelope. What she saw was something she couldn't ever imagine which was a letter from Tammy.

Hey Egypt:

Pick up ya mouth bitch. Yes it's your husband or are you still going to go forth with it? Look, I know that muthafucka Eric! He'll never change. Pussy is his downfall. Especially some white pussy! So get an eyeful of what years and years of your marriage will be like. Have a nice life.

Ha! Ha!
Tammy

Egypt couldn't believe it. "The nerve of this bitch Tammy and on my wedding day!" Egypt thought and glanced down at the pictures again. The sight of Eric fucking the white bitch she knew as Brooke, his new secretary was downright awful. But what really turned her stomach was him in between her legs eating her pussy. She stood up on that one and placed the contents back in the envelope. With a look that could kill written all over her face, she headed for the door.

"Girl where you going?" Tish asked.

"To see Eric!"

"You can't see him before the wedding. It's bad luck."

"Ain't going to be no wedding if he don't answer to this envelope!" she said and stormed off in the direction of the room that Eric was in.

Pretty E was adjusting his tie and suit jacket to his tux while brushing his hair in the mirror. "Damn!" he thought as he looked at himself, "I'm a sharp ass nigga!" He turned away from the mirror and looked at his nephew Jaquan, his best man and said, "Nephew my playing days is over. I never thought I'd say this, but Pretty E is dying today. I'm a lay that nigga to rest and bring Eric out," he spoke from the heart and really met it. Egypt was the love of his life. His first love and soul mate. The one who as a young teen helped him dream, dream of a future outside of the reality they were in, the Projects. And although Pretty E wasn't actually from the Projects, his heart was there because of his friends. He hated having and they didn't. That's why he chose to do what he did and hustled like Rasul, Dog, and Hit Man. Pretty E was determined to get his own and he did, they did, as a team with one common goal, "Get Rich or Die Trying". They did both, and he was the last man standing. "Yeah," he thought. "It's that time. Time to give it all up and grow old with my baby," he told himself, and then the door flew open.

"Eric! What da fuck is this?!" Egypt demanded.

"What?" he asked confused.

"Jaquan, excuse you! You too, and you too! All of y'all get da fuck out!" Egypt snapped again, and Jaquan and the groom's men all hurried out, leaving Pretty E and Egypt alone.

"Baby what da fuck is the matter? What's wrong?!"

"This is what's wrong! This shit right here is what's wrong!" Egypt cursed disregarding the fact that she was in a church. She slammed the manila envelope into his chest, stood with her arms crossed, and tapped her foot on the ground. "Well?!" she asked as he looked through the photos dumbfounded.

"Damn," Pretty E thought. "That's why the bitch quit," he said to himself as he looked at the photos and letter from Tammy. "Why would she do some shit like this after I let the bitch walk?" he questioned Tammy's doings. He didn't know where to begin. He was cold busted and couldn't have been more busted than if he was caught in the act.

"Well," Egypt asked again. "What's da matter? What you ain't got anything to say?" Pretty E didn't answer. He was trying to come up with the right shit to say to save his marriage because the wrong response would surely mean it's over.

"Look," he began then thought, "I'm a keep this shit all the way "G". Egypt I know these pictures look bad," he said as he tore them up. "But that's all they are, pictures. I'm not going to deny them because yes it's me. However, it was me prior to today. That person in those pictures was Pretty E. Today when we exchange our vows, that person dies, and Eric returns. The real Eric," he said moving in close to grab her in his arms. Standing in the middle of the room with his bride to be looking like an African Queen in her hand crafted bridal gown made by Roberta Cavali, he continued. "What I'm trying to say baby is this, when I say "I Do" in just a few minutes that's just what it means, "I Do": I do leave everything in the past behind me, I do stop cheating, I do stop lusting, I do become yours and only yours," he said staring into her eyes. She was softening up and he knew it. Now was the time to lay it on thick. "Baby I love you, love you with everything I got in me," he said and kissed her softly on the lips. "Now go on back in that other room, fix yourself up, and meet your husband up at that altar baby. We came too far for this."

"Eric," she tried to say.

"Shhhh. Don't say nuffin," he said and pecked her on the lips again. "Say it at the altar," he told her and led her out the door. "Don't make me wait," he said with a smile, and Egypt couldn't do anything but smile. That was her man and this was her day, and she'd be damn if she let Tammy steal her joy. "Bitch you just mad," she thought and went to get ready for her wedding. Pretty E sighed with relief.

■■■■■

🎵 *You and I / On Earth Together*
Say, Just You and I
God Has Sent Your Love To Me
My Friend
You and I / You and I /You and I

Stevie Wonder: "You and I"

Stevie Wonder sat at the head of the church on 7th and Walnut Street behind his grand piano and was singing his heart out like always. Pretty E had spent a grip to get him here today on a last second notice, but here he was, and the entire church was mesmerized at the sound of his voice and the sight of him rocking back and forth, his movements almost hypnotizing. Pretty E stood before the altar and looked down the aisle at his bride being walked down to him by her father. Mr. Wright was dapper in his Pierre Hardy suit, compliments of Pretty E, and he knew it as he handed his daughter's hand in marriage to Pretty E.

Pretty E took Egypt's hand into his and gave her the proudest smile she ever seen. He was actually gleaming almost glowing with a shine she had never seen before and knew then that Eric "Pretty E" Williams met every word he said back there in the room. There wasn't a doubt in her mind that he wasn't a changed man. "I love you," he said to her and used his thumb to wipe the running eyeliner from her face but it only smudged it.

"Baby, that's Stevie Wonder!"

"I know. I did it for you baby," he said and the preacher began.

"Dearly beloved we are gathered here today to join this man, Eric Williams, and this woman, Egypt Wright in holy matrimony," he started out. He said a few more things then asked for the rings and Pretty E and Egypt went into their own written vows. Egypt went first.

"Eric," she said reading from a paper. "From as long as I can remember I dreamed for this day. This is the day that all little girls dream of, the day they become married. The day they get to get all dressed up in front of everybody they know to proclaim their love to the man of their dreams. And Eric baby you are mine," she cried. "From the day I met you in

Riverside sitting on the Project steps, to the nights we spent looking up at the sky while we laid back on the green boxes, I knew you were going to be my husband. Eric Williams I love you, and I thought I lost you back when I was in college at the University of Southern Cal, but the saying is true. If it's true love, it will come back and baby here we are. It is my pleasure to become Mrs. Eric Williams. Eric, do you accept me as your bride?"

"I do," he said and she slid the wedding band on his finger. A single tear fell from behind his Dolce & Gabbana shades. He wiped it away with the back of his hand.

"Eric your ring and vows," the preacher said.

"Egypt," Pretty E began by holding her hand and the ring up to the tip of her finger. He pulled his vows from his inside jacket pocket and started to read from the paper but crumbled it up. A few "Dat's rights!" and "Take ya times" were shouted out along with some claps as Pretty E shot the balled up piece of paper in the trash can. "Baby fuck dat paper," he started out then apologized for cursing in the church. "I'm sorry y'all. I forgot where we were at, but love can make you do that. Baby, my baby, my boo, my poopie-stinkers, my soul mate, my other half, my wife, my everything, I love you. Baby you helped me get my life back. You stood by my side and fought the disease of addiction with me. You made me realize that drugs created even more problems. I thought that the high from drugs was incomparable to anything in the world until I ran back into you at detox baby. I realized then that there wasn't a high in the world like a "bag of Egypt". Once I tried a bag of you, I've been back in my active addiction every since," he smiled. "Egypt, Pretty E is no longer. He's dead as of today and Eric is born. Eric Williams, the one my parents raised, not the one whose characteristic traits were created by the streets. That shit was all false baby," he took his shades off. "I want the world to see how I feel for you girl!!" he shouted and tears began to pour out of his eyes. Egypt threw her hand over her mouth and cried at the sight of Pretty E's tears, and then he continued, "Egypt, it is an honor to me that you are standing here with me. And it's my pleasure to ask you to be my wife. Baby there are only two things in this world that I ain't seen, and that's an UFO, and a woman as beautiful as you. Egypt Wright, will you marry me? Please baby, say I do," he said to her.

"Baby I do!" She cried.

"Ladies and gentlemen," the preacher began. "I present to you Mr. and Mrs. Eric Williams," he turned to Pretty E and said," You may now kiss your bride," he announced and the church erupted in applause, as Pretty E and Egypt shared a two minute kiss at the head of the church, and Stevie Wonder played, "These Three Words". It was time for the reception now and Pretty E couldn't wait for his first dance with his wife. He also had a surprise up his sleeve. He was going to sing "Pretty Brown Eyes" by Mint Condition to her. He had been practicing all month long. So now as the people filed out of the church and took their places outside, and lined the steps. Pretty picked up his wife and walked out the church with her cradled in his arms. Cheers of joy went off by the people as they threw rice and confetti in the air. Pretty E and Egypt's wedding was one to remember. It was going to go down in the history books.

■■■■■

🎵 *Many Men / Wish Death Upon Me*
Blood In My Eye / Dog Now You Goin See
I'm Trying To Be / What I'm Destined To Be
But Niggaz Trying Take My Life Away
I Put A Hole In A Nigga / For Fuckin Wit Me
My Back On The Wall / Dog You Goin See
Better Watch How You Talk / When You Talk About Me
Cause I'll Come And Take Ya Life Away
Many Men / Many / Many / Many / Many / Men

50 Cent: "Many Men"
(Get Rich or Die Trying)

Tammy gave them the time and date of the wedding at Greater Bethel on Walnut Street, and they were there. "Zoned Out" and anticipating what was about to happen next as 50 Cent pounded through the "Hurst" speakers as Tommy Good and Mike Cottman waited patiently only a block away from the wedding. Pretty E was a sitting duck and they knew it. Tammy had kept Tommy posted on everything. She told him how the police had eased up, the latest on what people were saying, and where everybody thought they were at, and so Tommy and Mike knew he'd never suspect the unexpected. Then the church doors opened up. Mike hit the gas.

∎∎∎∎∎

Pretty E took each step cautiously as he carried Egypt to the awaiting Rolls Royce at the bottom of the church steps. Being slightly paralyzed took time now, but he was almost there. Almost to the car with the "Just Married" markings all over the back window when out of the corner of his eye, he saw the black celebrity creeping. Instantly, everything moved in slow motion. It was as if his shoes were made of concrete because he couldn't move. He was frozen with fear, and then out jumped Tommy Good and Mike Cottman.

"Pop! Pop! Pop! Pop! Pop! Pop!"

"Boom! Boom! Boom! Boom! Boom!"

Mike's twin .45 caliber pistols, and Tommy's .357 magnums erupted into the air and through the crowd in front of the church striking several people. A barrage of bullets went off again, only this time they hit its target as they watched Pretty E fall down still carrying his wife.

Shit was happening so fast that it took some time for Jaquan and his crew, along with Lil Frankie and some of the Capellis to react. Tommy and Mike had done something totally unexpected. But when the bullets started flying back in their direction, they jumped back in the "Hurst" and pulled off speeding down Walnut St. and disappearing down 9th Street. When the smoke cleared, all that could be heard was the loud cries and sobs of Pretty E. In his arms he was holding his beautiful queen dressed in her fairytale, white gown that now had a huge burgundy stain, blood stain, in the front of it and blood pouring out the corner of her mouth. Egypt had just lost her life.

Chapter Sixteen

At the Philadelphia International Airport, Ann paced the floor back and forth with the kids. Their flight to Brazil would be there in less than an hour and there were still no signs of Mike and Tommy anywhere. "Where are they at?" she thought before finally taking a seat exhausted from pacing the floor. She had no idea that right now she was under major surveillance by the FBI. They were tipped about the shooting in Delaware, so they set up at all major outlets leading out of the state. Toll booths, bus stations, train stations, and airports from Baltimore, Maryland to New York City. They struck gold in Philly and set up the largest ambush and surveillance stakeout in the East Coast history. Tommy Good and Mike Cottman wouldn't get out of this one.

"I have the suspect, Mrs. Ann Cottman in plain view captain," one agent said into his hidden microphone.

"Ok number ten. Don't lose her."

"I won't."

■■■■■■

"I'll shoot your mom's house up and make ya ass look for me," 50 Cent sang as Mike jumped on 495 passing Gander Hill on the way. He and Tommy were headed to the airport to leave the country, but only after this last mission, the mission to kill Robin, Raven's twin.

"Are you sure she still lives in the house I bought off of Fitz for Raven?" Tommy asked finding the key on his ring.

"Yeah, I'm positive."

"Well look," Tommy began as he looked at his watch. "We got plenty of time bruh. Let's go handle this broad then hit the airport and tonight nigga we'll be in Brazil," Tommy assured him.

"Fo 'sho!" Mike agreed and got off on the South Street exit.

■■■■■

Since Robin offered "Fajr" prayer this morning, something was weighing heavy on her heart and mind, she just couldn't pinpoint it. It was bothering her so much that she made "Dua" and read iyats from her noble Quran day, even in some of her classes until Allah finally started to ease her burden. Being as though this was her day off from work, she decided to go down to Center City to the "Gallery" before going home. She had a taste for a Ms. Annie's cinnamon & sugar dipped pretzel and nothing was stopping her from getting it. So now as she pinched piece after piece of the pretzel off from out of the white and blue bag she carried, she was heading home. The heavy burden from earlier, her school work, and now this walk from the Gallery to her home had her drained. She was ready for a nap. Robin walked into her home stepping through the doorway with her foot first, something the Prophet Muhammad used to do, and kicked off her shoes. "Ooo Du Be Lah He Men A Shaitan A Rhazeem," she said, meaning "Oh Allah, I seek refuge in you from the accursed Satan," and headed off into the shower.

■■■■■■

Tommy and Mike saw her go in and got out of the "Hurst". They stepped quickly up to the house because they were pressed for time. Their flight left in a little over a half hour from now, so they knew this had to be a quick job. Deciding that South Street was not the ideal spot to commit a murder they ruled, they put away their guns. Because the first time a shot would go off, police would be there before they made it out of the door. So Tommy decided to choke her out.

Putting his key into the lock of the house, it opened just like Raven's did. He couldn't understand for the life of him why they wouldn't change the locks after he died, but he was glad they hadn't, especially right now.

Tommy and Mike entered the house and headed straight to what they heard, the shower running. Robin was upstairs taking a shower. "Perfect," Tommy thought. He tiptoed up the stairs and stood outside the door and waited, when he heard the water stop. She was on her way out.

■■■■■■

Robin stepped out of the shower and dried off as she stood before the mirror. "Hello! Who is dat?!" she called out, but no one answered. "I'm hearing things," she told herself. The house was just too quiet. She knew she should've turned on the radio. Wrapping her hair up in one towel and her body in another, Robin turned the knob on the bathroom door to leave. As soon as she stepped out, her nightmare came true, the nightmare of Tommy Good strangling her to death.

"Aaaahhhh!" she screamed at the top of her lungs, but Tommy caught it in her throat. His hands felt like vices around her neck as she struggled to get free. Mike wanted to help. He wanted to get the shit over and done with fast. And since they weren't using guns, he clutched the handle on his machete waiting to swing it.

"Bitch!" Tommy spat. "What you thought you was just going to get away with that bullshit?!" he asked as he watched her eyes bulge out of the sockets, then she kneed him in the balls. Tommy lost his grip, and she darted for her room to try and lock the door, but Tommy grabbed her foot causing her to fall. He leaped on top of her. Fighting for her life, the towel around her body managed to come off and there she laid naked, kicking, and screaming trying to get away.

Mike's heart began to pound in his chest the more she screamed and fought to get away. He clutched his machete even tighter now as her screams and cries started to do something to him. They flipped him into his subconscious mind and instantly Robin's face became Michelle's, his twin sister. He tried to wipe his eyes and shake the thoughts from his head, but when he opened them, Tommy had become the Deacon. The entire rape of Michelle was playing out right before Mike's eyes. He screamed, "Noooo! Get off of my sister!" like a scared little boy and in one swift motion swung the machete, taking Tommy's head clean off his shoulders. His lifeless body shook from nerves on top of Robin as she lay motionless. She was in a state of shock, as Mike snatched Tommy's body from off of hers.

"Michelle it's ok, ok? I got that muthafucka. He can never hurt you again. Get dressed. I'm going to get mommy and tell her you're ok," Mike said as if talking to his sister. Robin was lost. She had no idea what Mike was talking about, but she sure was thanking Allah for blessing her with her life. Mike looked down at the headless body at his feet, and then to the head that was once attached, and kicked it clean down the hallway. Robin balled up in the corner covered in blood and pulled her knees up into her body, as the man she knew as Mike left the house. When he was gone she reached for the phone and called the police.

■■■■■■

Mike ran out of the house with the bloody machete still in his hand. Up the sidewalk, between people, he ran towards the "Hurst" and jumped in. The people were petrified as he ran towards them with the sword hanging in his hand, so they just stepped to the side, none wanting any conflict with the man that had a crazed look in his eye. Mike turned the key to the ignition and the "Hurst" came to life. He headed towards the airport to Ann. He had a flight to catch. Then it dawned on him as he drove down the highway with an empty passenger seat that Tommy wasn't with him. "What have I done?!" Mike asked himself when reality set in. He killed his boy Tommy Good.

Ann saw Mike heading her way, but Tommy was nowhere in sight. She looked up at the board then heard the announcement over the intercom that the flight to Brazil was now boarding at Gate Four. Mike had made it just in time.

"Where's Tommy at?" she asked her husband, but sensed something wrong. The look on his face told it all, and then a tear fell from his eye. That was the first time she seen him cry since his sister's funeral, so she knew it had to be bad. She decided to leave well enough alone and took him into her arms. She began to tell him that it was ok and everything was going to be alright as he cried harder. The sobs and sniffles she heard in her ears made her cry too. "Come on baby," she said. "We have a flight to catch."

■■■■■■

"Yes. We got 'em. Let's move in!! Move out! Move out! Move out!!" the lead captain of the FBI task force said, and they moved in like swat.

Mike and Ann never saw it coming. The only thing they knew was that they were being taken into custody by the FBI. It was like a media frenzy as John Walsh and his production crew of America's Most Wanted swarmed in behind the Feds. Mike and Ann put their heads down and remained silent as they were escorted to awaiting Suburbans and Durangos outside in the airport's terminal. Their sons were taken into custody by the Division of Child Services and would later be turned over to Raven and Ann's mom. But as for now, Mike and Ann were in for a long day, and a whole lot of questioning.

"You have the right to remain silent," the captain began reading them their Miranda rights as they pulled off from the airport to FDC in Center City Philadelphia, nick named the "Cheeze Factory" on the streets from all the rats. For some reason, Mike knew that his life was over.

■■■■■■

For the next sixteen or more hours, the Feds questioned Mike and Ann for hours on in about everything from drugs, to homicides, to assets, and estates. They had pictures, written testimonies, documents, and whatever else they needed to build a case against them, but they weren't breaking, not Ann nor Mike. They were surprised at her composure. Even when they threatened her with her kids she wouldn't move an inch. "Take 'em muthafucka! They'll be well taken care of! Believe dat!" she would say. Her response was one they hadn't heard before.

"Ok smart ass," the captain said. "We'll just do that then."

"Fuck you!" she replied then was escorted to her cell for the tenth time. The Feds had a way of doing that. They would take you out and put you in a cell so many different times it would drive you crazy. It was a tactic they used to intimidate you, or break you, but Ann wasn't falling for it. She knew the games they played. So as she lay back on her steel bunk in a solitaire confined room, she counted the bricks on the walls until she fell asleep. "Fuck you pigs!" she thought with a smile. She knew she was going home. Mike was going to make sure of it.

■■■■■■

In another part of the prison sitting in a room surrounded by Feds at a table with a tape recorder in front of him, Mike started his confessions.

"State your name please," the agent conducting the taping said.

"Michael "Mike" Cottman," he said and began a tale so gruesome that some of the agents covered their ears. The man who was sitting before them could have easily been a real life Jason Voorhees or Michael Myers. He showed no emotion as he gave them details of countless amounts of murders he committed over the years, dating back to the early days from 27th and Market St. to Hollywood. He told of the kilos and kilos of cocaine he sold all the way down to the connects he killed for them. He even gave up the address to the house where Boomer, Zy, and Peacock were buried at. He gave them all the information they asked of him, except when it pertained to someone else. A rat was something he wasn't, but he did tell on himself, even lied about the five bodies found burned in his house, and he did it all for Ann. The Feds promised to release Ann the minute the confession was over. Four hours and twenty minutes later, the agent stopped the tape. They had Mike Cottman where they wanted him. Then a call from the front came through and they stood Mike in front of the mirror. He knew on the other side stood someone, but he had no idea who it could've been, he had done so much dirt. The person on the other side positively I.D.'d Mike as the killer and was escorted away. The way Robin had explained what happened at her house today when all this was taking place had Detective Cohen and the Federal agents who were investigating the case baffled. The way she said Mike was acting and calling her a girl named "Michelle" had them thinking that at the time he was committing the act he was in a state of delusion, had somehow fallen out of consciousness for just that moment and fell into a state of delirium. The more she talked, the more they tried to understand their perpetrator, Mike Cottman. Confused, they dug deeper into a past that they would eventually dread. What they found out about Mike Cottman made

Detective Cohen and every agent, especially the main agent, Lt. McMichelson, wish they never did. "Shit!" Lt. McMichelson said and slammed his fists into the stack of files that lay before him. "That's all we needed," he said to Detective Cohen.

"What?" he asked.

"This," McMichelson said passing him the file of Mike Cottman's medical and psychological history.

Detective Cohen's mouth dropped to the floor when he read the papers before him. Mike Cottman had been diagnosed with a paranoid schizophrenia and labeled legally insane by professionals' years ago. The papers also read that he had been receiving checks from the State of Delaware for being disabled and had been prescribed and taking "psych meds" Thorazine and Trazodone for anti-depression. He was also on Seraquil. With a history and past like that, the officers knew that there was a good chance that with a good lawyer, Mike Cottman wouldn't do a day in jail. They'd go for an insanity plea bargain right off the back on the day of his arraignment and the thought of him walking just didn't sit right with them. Instead of jail, he'd do time at a mental institution like the State Hospital, which was actually like still having your freedom. This was one time it paid to be crazy. They just hoped that the D.A. prosecuting the case would be good enough to somehow convince the jury into a "Guilty" verdict for 1st degree Capital Murder for the decapitation of Thomas "Tommy" Good. With the confession tape, the skeletal remains of three bodies; Zy, Boomer, and Peacock in an abandoned house he owned on 8th and Franklin St., and all the other murders he admitted to, they were sure he'd get the death penalty if convicted. They just prayed on their lucky stars that the jurors would disregard the fact that Mike was mentally insane.

"Let's just cross our fingers," McMichelson said.

"Yeah," Detective Cohen agreed. "I second that notion."

Chapter Seventeen

The day after Pretty E's wedding and the death of his wife Egypt, clear up to the day he put her in the ground nearly a week later he fell into a state of depression so severe that he became mute. He hadn't spoken a word and that's what worried people the most, especially Jaquan. Pretty E was all he had left of the people he loved the most. His mother, Tameeka, stepfather, Rasul, Uncle Dog and Hit Man had all lost their lives too soon, leaving him to be a man at an age way too early. He nearly lost Pretty E too, to a drug addiction that he overcame and life was just beginning to return to normal, now this. Jaquan's biggest fear was that he'll lose his uncle again to a severe relapse in addiction. That's why him and his new girlfriend, Tamira, the one that he met on New Year's at her son, and son's father Greeny's funeral spent at least two or three hours daily with him trying to encourage him to come out of the shell he was in. Tamira was just the help and companion that Jaquan needed. By her being there at his side to tend to Lil Tameeka, and Pretty E's son Rasul Hakeem while he handled business, took a lot of slack off of him and he was able to focus on his uncle more. Within weeks Pretty E was talking again.

"So what's up Unc? What's on ya mind today?" Jaquan asked him as he picked at the plate of food Tamira had prepared for him.

"Ain't shit man. Just trying to put all this shit in perspective so I can make sense out of it all, you know? I miss my mufuckin babe. Tammy fucked my life up. Everything that has happened to us was because of that bitch you call your aunt. She told dat nigga Tommy Good our every move," Pretty E told his nephew as he looked on confused. He had no idea that Tammy, his mother's best friend had been the one responsible for the deaths of his loved ones.

"Damn," Jaquan uttered.

"Yeah nephew, damn is right. That bitch is grimy as shit. I'm just trying to figure out now how to get at her. That bitch gotta go."

"Damn," Jaquan repeated.

"So what's up wit 'chu? Where's Tamira at? How y'all coming along?" Pretty E asked him and he brightened up at the mentioning of her name. "Oh it's that good huh?" Pretty E teased his nephew before he could answer.

"Man stop dat shit," Jaquan said still smiling heavily. "Yeah Unc, its going that good. I'm thinking about marrying her."

"Oh yeah?"

"Yeah that's my baby," Jaquan assured him about Tamira, the woman he thought he knew. If only he would've known who she really was behind that beautiful face and centerfold body, he might not have thought about considering marriage. Tamira was a stone cold killer who'd kill again at the drop of a hat, and she would. It was just a matter of time.

"Well if that's what you want to do I'm wit 'chu. You know that right?"

"Yeah."

"Ok then let me get ready to go to bed cause a nigga tired, feel me?"

"Damn what 'chu rushing me off?"

"Nah nephew. I just got a big day ahead of me tomorrow," he said because he had made up his mind. Remembering the day of Egypt's funeral, and seeing the "white doves" fly off into the sky after releasing them from the cage, he decided to kill her. Ready and prepared to deal with whatever came down the pipe after killing this bitch Tammy. He just couldn't live with the guilt he was living with anymore, something had to give. And after his nephew left, Pretty E sat the picture of him and his wife on their wedding day kissing down on the table and stared at it. The next morning, bright and early he got out of bed and went downstairs to look at the picture again. Standing still in the middle of his living room floor, he took in a mental note and picture of his once happy home and etched it in his mind forever. Next, he grabbed his keys to his car, the package from FedEx addressed to Egypt with the pictures of him she received on her wedding day, and left out the door. He looked back over his shoulder one more time at his home because he might not ever see it again.

■■■■■■

The sun's rays fought their way through a crack in the blinds of the bedroom window and found its resting place right in the middle of Tammy's face. She squinted her eyes, pulled the sheet up over her face and rolled over, scooting up next to Monique who was at her side balled up in a fetal position. Wrapping her arms around

Monique, Tammy pulled her body close to hers until Monique's butt fit perfectly into her stomach. They fit together like pieces to a puzzle. Tammy stayed that way for the next fifteen to twenty minutes trying to go back to sleep, but the cuddling did nothing for her this morning. She was wide awake. So after realizing that sleep was out of the question, she decided to get up, get out, and get something. Tammy walked down the steps to her new half a million dollar home, courtesy of Relax Sinsations and opened up the front door to check the weather out. Today was going to be a good day she knew because right at 8:30 in the morning the temperature was in the low to high 80s. That wasn't the only reason it was going to be a good day either, it was going to be a good day because the parlor was booked with clients today, clients who all wanted full body massages and other extra-curricular activities. By the end of the day at closing time, the parlor should see a fifteen to twenty thousand dollar day.

"Good morning baby, why you just standing in the doorway like that?" Monique asked her when she came downstairs.

"Good morning. I was just seeing what it was like outside that's all. What are you doing up?" Tammy asked her.

"You know I can't sleep if you're not in bed with me," Monique told her and hugged her from behind. "You hungry?"

"A little bit."

"Well let me go make us something to eat," Monique said and walked in the direction of the kitchen.

After they were done the quick breakfast of pancakes, eggs, and bacon that Monique prepared, they headed for the shower to get dressed. A few moments later they were out feeling fresh and ready to route. Today was just going to be one of those days, Tammy felt it.

Monique checked the house to make sure the flat irons were unplugged, the alarm was set, and all the doors were locked. Once she knew that everything was cool, she headed to the basement and through the side door of the house into the garage where Tammy was waiting in their new convertible 650 Beemer. Tammy hit the "Genie" garage door opener and backed out the driveway and into the street. She hit the converter and the top slowly began to drop on the car. The sun shown down on the marble white paint with the pink swirls in it making it look as though it was pink when the sun hit it a certain way, and the white seats piped in pink stitching complimented everything about the machine. Tammy mashed the gas pedal admiring the power of the car, and the faster she went, the more her and Monique's hair blew in the wind as they watched the world go by through the lenses of their "Chanel" framed shades. Tammy looked into the rear view mirror at herself, and then to Monique at her side and said, "Bitch if we ain't Hollywood then what are we?" she asked Monique with a smile, and then high-fived her.

For Tammy, life couldn't be going better. She was one of the most successful business women in the state of Delaware. She had been granted a pardon wiping her record clean of everything she ever did, and she was engaged to be married to Monique next year. Yes, she finally admitted it; Tammy was full blown lesbian thanks to Pretty E. The way he did her all those years had her convinced. She didn't want no parts of anymore dick. As far as Pretty E was concerned, she was happy at the way things turned out for him at the hands of Tommy Good. Once again he was miserable and alone, and from what she heard, he was back getting high. "Wallow in dat shit nigga!" Tammy said to herself at the thought. "I told you nigga, don't ever cross me. I always get the last laugh," she chuckled under her breath, and then Monique asked, "What's so funny?"

"Nuffin baby I was just thinking about something that's all."

"What?" Monique was persistent.

"Girl you ain't right. That man has had a terrible string of bad luck," Monique said clueless to the fact that everything that ever happened to him was a result of Tammy's doings.

"Well you know the saying: Sometimes you get the bear, and sometimes the bear gets you!" and she laughed her ass off as she pressed the gas pedal a little harder. Having Pretty E fucked up and miserable was all that mattered to her. And right now, the way his life was going, she finally decided to leave well enough alone and move on with her life. She had been the demise of Pretty E and that's all she wanted.

For the rest of the morning Tammy and Monique enjoyed a light pampering at the nail salon getting their hands and feet manicured and pedicured. They then enjoyed a stroll through the Wal-Mart picking up a few household products before heading to the parlor. Monique had a twelve o' clock appointment with none other than Detective Cohen, a senior vice officer who had been trying to bust Pretty E for years. Today just might be his lucky day.

■■■■■■

Outside of Relax Sinsations only a block away, Pretty E sat in his Asti Martin smoking Newport after Newport while he stared at the front door of the establishment he brought for this ungrateful bitch Tammy. The "game" and the streets of life had him smoking his squares by the cartons, but "so what" he thought. If he didn't die from the disease cancer, he was going to die of a broken heart anyway. So just like that, he lit up yet another one, his fifth one in twenty minutes, and let the smoke escape his body through his nose.

The longer he sat outside, the easier his thoughts became about what he was about to do. Especially when he noticed how the world was still going on and his had stopped and no one seemed to notice or care. Right now as he sat in his car, his heart was broken. Nearly all his loved ones, Lucy, Dog, Hit Man, Rasul, and now Egypt had all passed away and people were just a smiling and laughing as they went on with their lives like nothing ever happened. That was the reason right there that he decided to do what he was going to do today. Because no one seemed to care, not even him anymore.

Pretty E had to have been sitting out there for at least two hours now. He watched the front door intensely as man after man entered the parlor and left with a smile being escorted out and walked to their car by one of the women working inside. He saw Chyna, Snow White, Blondie, Flame, and Slim at least twice a piece escort a man out to his car, hug him, and kiss him on the cheek before they pulled off and realized for the first time how much of a multi-billion dollar industry the business of pussy was. It would go unnoticed if you didn't look at it because pussy is free to most of us. However, there are some people who have to pay for pussy. We, the ones who don't, sometimes even tend to pay for pussy. It was just a male thing to do. If you are reading this right now and thinking: "Not me! I'll never pay for pussy!" think again. That pocketbook, that outfit, them shoes, that hairdo, them nails, that electric bill you paid or brought for that other girl that wasn't the wife, yeah, consider next time looking at the receipt because guess what, you just brought some pussy!!! Now back to the story. (Smile) ☺.

Anyway, Pretty E was getting "antsy" just sitting there, and was thinking about leaving and coming back, but as soon as he was about to turn the key on the ignition he saw the 650 pull up. It was now or never.

■■■■■■

Detective Cohen was on time as usual on his day off today and ready for the first of his twice a month full body massage at Relax Sinsations by Monique. The twice a month massage was something he treated himself to that he kept to himself. His wife would probably kill him if she knew about this little secret, not to mention the pussy and blow job he paid for when his money permitted it. Like today, he was getting all that and his dick was hard at the thought of it. Detective Cohen saw when Monique pulled up and walked into the parlor. He checked his car, locked the doors, and was getting ready to head on in himself when he saw Pretty E walking into the parlor before him. The way he looked caused Detective Cohen to stop in his tracks. It was something wrong with the picture. Pretty E wasn't looking like himself. His face was unshaved, he looked twenty pounds lighter, and he was in desperate need of a haircut. But what really had Detective Cohen in wonderment were his eyes. Pretty E looked like his soul had long left his body.

■■■■■

The massage parlor was packed like it always was on Saturdays, which made Tammy and all the employees happy as they bounced around the inside gingerly. Relax Sinsations was in full stride and filled with a lot of prominent men throughout the community, which made for a very profitable day. Mark and Bough, the two young bails bondsmen were there. Leondrei Prince was there. He was the one responsible for bringing to the readers who loved to read the Publishing Company, L. Prince Presents. You had the overseas star basketball player Tone Washam there, even the local rapper whose song "Socks In Da Air Waves Jumpin", Shizz Nitty was there. However, the real big dogs were the few judges that were there and two of the top young brokers in the business, Lamar Gunn and his protégé J.R. Tammy greeted them all with a smile then took her seat behind the desk in the main lobby. "Hello everyone!" she gleamed and every man there wished that Tammy herself was their therapist. They all wanted a piece of the caramel colored beauty with the body like "Jackie O".

"Hello Tammy!" they all said in unison, sounding like a chorus, which made everyone laugh. That was the good thing about Relax Sinsations, the togetherness, because it made you feel a little more comfortable about what you were doing. The "something like family" atmosphere made the act of prostitution less troubling on the mind. The customers felt right at home.

"How is everyone today?" she asked.

"We're good," one of the judges spoke for all of them.

"That's nice to know. I'm glad that we at Relax Sinsations can accommodate you to your liking," she said and in walked Pretty E.

Pretty E saw her beautiful smile the minute he walked through the door. That was one of her assets, her pure white teeth that were perfectly straight. Her smile could have easily been placed on the side of a Colgate box, but to Pretty E right now, it looked evil, almost sinister. He couldn't believe how bright and full of energy and life she was. Here it was she was living her life without a care in the world, like she hadn't done one thing bad in her life, reaping all the benefits of a successful business, and Pretty E couldn't even function in life anymore. He had given up that day, the day his wife died in his arms on that church step.

Tammy saw him come in, but couldn't believe how he looked. The sight of him scared her a little bit because he looked crazy, like he had lost his mind. Tammy had never seen him look this way; even in his worst addiction he didn't look this bad. His hair was knotty and full of lint, his face was unshaven and also full of lint, his face hadn't been washed, she could tell by the coal in the corner of his eyes, and he looked skinny as hell. He walked up to her desk and took the photos of him and Brooke having sex out of the FedEx package along with her letter to Egypt. Tammy's eyes widened and a look like she didn't know what was going on crossed her face. Next he took his wife's obituary and tossed it on her desk. Then he leaned in forward and let his hands rest on her desk while holding himself up. Everything in Relax Sinsations came to a standstill, and all eyes were on them. As he leaned in closer, Tammy leaned back further in her seat. She didn't know what this crazed person in front of her was about to do, but then he smiled and shook his head at her in pity almost, disgusted that she could even pretend what she did to him hadn't happened.

"Damn Tammy," Pretty E began, "you know I really can't believe how you could do me like this you dig?"

"What are you talking about? Boy you is crazy!" she said with a straight face. Pretty E chuckled.

"You are dead serious huh?" Pretty E asked. "You really going to sit up here and act like you ain't have nothing to do with me ending up like this huh. I just put the pictures, your letter, and my wife's obituary on the desk. Look!!" he began to get upset with her denial and straight face. "The shit is in ya face!"

"I didn't have anything to do with your wife getting killed Eric, and I'm sorry it happened. But hey, what you want me to do?" she said real nonchalantly and in a flash, like a snake striking, Pretty E reached and grabbed her throat and put the pistol to the side of her head as he talked.

"He has a gun!" one of the men yelled out creating a brief commotion that was quickly seized. "Pow!" the nine millimeter sounded, as a bullet tore into the ceiling causing a slight downpour of drywall.

"Shut da fuck up and sit da fuck down!" Pretty E began as smoke still oozed from the barrel of the gun. He placed the hot steel back to the side of her head and said, "you see this bitch right here?!" he didn't wait for a response, "this is the type of bitch that doesn't deserve to live. The type of muthafucka that is so slimy, death is the only option for them. I don't know why, but this bitch right here has made it her duty to make my life hell! Even after I let this bitch walk for trying to kill me! I have done things for this woman that I haven't done for my own mother, and she repays me like this!" he stopped to breathe and hold up the obituary of Egypt for all to see. Then he began again. "I'm the reason y'all are standing and sitting up in this muthafucking establishment! I bought this muthafucking building for her. I took care of her because I loved her. But she goes and repays me like this!" he said letting the obituary fall back on the desk. "Pick it up bitch!" he said to Tammy directly this time. "Pick it da fuck up! You see that beautiful woman on there that was my wife, and I lost her because of you!"

"Eric what are you talking about?" Tammy cried as she looked at the obituary in her hand.

"Shut da fuck up! Bitch, you know good and damn well what I'm talking about. Why Tammy? Why would you do that to me?" he said looking at her in her eyes sincerely. "Damn boo; do you hate me that much? Did I really do you that bad that you had to do me like this?" he asked her as a single tear fell from his eye. The sight of it made Tammy question herself, "damn did he really deserve all of that?" and no matter how much she wanted to say he did, the fact remained that she was just some jealous bitch whose pride got caught in the way. Now she was about to pay for it.

"Huh?" Pretty E asked her when she didn't respond. "See that's what I'm talking about. You can't even be honest, but it's ok. I know the deal. At first I didn't want to believe it, but after going over it again and again in my mind, the only answer to my questions why and how were you. It was just too coincidental that the nigga Tommy Good always appeared at the oddest times. Then I remembered that you were fucking that nigga! You told him about Rasul at the cemetery, you sent him to my wedding, and you kept him posted on my every move.

"Eric I would never," she tried to lie, but Pretty E cut her off.

"Shut da fuck up! Bitch you did do it!" he said through clenched teeth and slanted eyes as his nose flared up. "You know what though you won't live to do another muthafucka dirty," he said, smiled, then pulled the trigger. "Pop! Pop! Pop! Pop! Pop! Pop!" he unloaded the rest of the clip into Tammy's face. The sight of what the bullets did to her once perfect face was so gruesome and nasty; looking at it caused even some of the men present to throw up. Tammy's face was unrecognizable. Her nose was gone, her forehead was caved in, and her left cheek was gone making that side of her face look like Two-Face from the movie "Dark Knight". Tammy was fucked up and lying in a pool of blood that had formed underneath her head while she lay dead with a half of a smile. Monique's screams were deafening.

Standing over top of her lifeless body a relief overcame him and the weight of the world was lifted from his shoulders. Pretty E was at peace again in his own psychotic way because he'd never be normal again. He reached down, grabbed a fistful of Tammy's hair and drug her through the parlor like a caveman and straight out the front door for all to see. The sight of him dragging this dead woman down the Market St. mall towards his car caused women to scream and holler at the top of their lungs, but their cries fell on deaf ears. Pretty E didn't hear anything, except himself saying, "I need a cigarette," and that's what he went to get. Pretty E laid Tammy in front of his car, grabbed his Newport from inside the car, and sat down on his hood. With one foot on his bumper and the other one on Tammy's chest and breast, he lit up a Newport and waited for the police. He heard the sirens in the distance.

■■■■■

Detective Cohen heard the first shot go off and called for backup. Next, he pulled his gun from his shoulder holster and eased up on the building. When he got in eyes view of what was happening inside, he took aim at the suspect, Pretty E who was holding Tammy at gunpoint. He knew the history of the two; however he was clueless as to what was going on now. He wanted to take a shot at him, put one right in the back of his head for his partner, Detective Armstrong, but it was just too many pedestrians and innocent bystanders in the way for him to get a clear shot. "Oh how I want to pull this trigger," he thought to himself. "Then they'd all be dead 'ol buddy," he talked to Detective Armstrong like he was there. Then more shots rang out. He took cover. The next thing he saw was Pretty E dragging out the body of Tammy.

"Eric! Eric Williams!" Detective Cohen shouted out to Pretty E as he sat on the hood of his car smoking the cigarette. "Put the gun down now!" he yelled at the top of his lungs.

For a split second Pretty E thought about raising it in the direction of Detective Cohen and committing suicide by cop, but went against it. There was no way he was giving Detective Cohen that gratification or Tammy for that matter. "Fuck dat! I'm keeping my life," he thought.

"Eric put da gun down!" Detective Cohen shouted again and Pretty E obliged. He popped the clip from the gun, laid both it and the gun down next to Tammy, and stood up. Taking a long drag from his Newport and filled his lungs up with the smoke, Pretty E turned, plucked the burning remains of the cigarette down into the mesh that was once her beautiful face, and then put his arms straight up into the air. After that he turned his back to Detective Cohen with his arms still pointed towards the sky and got down on his knees before lying flat out on his stomach. Detective Cohen rushed him the moment he saw him lie flat out in his most vulnerable point and slammed his knees down into the small of his back and cuffed his arms behind his back. When he turned him over to face him and read him his rights, Detective Cohen knew then that this wasn't the same man he had been after since his juvenile days. In his eyes he saw a man who was distant. A man defeated. Pretty E had given up on life and lost his own life in the spiritual aspect of it the day he laid his wife, Egypt to rest.

"Eric Williams you are under arrest. You have the right to remain silent. You have the right to an attorney," Detective Cohen began and Pretty E burst out into a laugh of a 'Mad Man', a man whose mind was completely insane. Then he began to cry and then broke out into a laugh again. Pretty E was gone. It was going to take plenty of medication, the asylum, and hours and hours of lying down on the huge leather sofa being counseled by a shrink telling you shit you already knew. Before Pretty E could even begin to think about regaining his sanity, if he did at all, all those things would have to be done. As for now Pretty E was "coo coo" for Cocoa Puffs and three sandwiches away from a picnic.

"Damn shame," thought Detective Cohen.

Chapter Eighteen

The federal courthouse on 8th and King St. was a media frenzy today as one of Wilmington's and the entire East Coast clean down to the Bayous of Louisiana most notorious drug kingpin was having a preliminary hearing today on drugs, weapons, money-laundering, and murder charges. Michael "Mike" Cottman and his wife Ann's team of attorneys would today hear what evidence the United States government had against them and, the courtroom was unbelievably packed on this sunny July day. The press stood around the courtroom walls as pedestrians filled the seats along with family members of both the Cottmans' and the Goods', and all of the other murder victims' families and friends. It seemed as though they all were there and full of courage now that Tommy Good was really dead and Mike Cottman was in custody because before this they'd never show up in a courtroom against either of them, Tommy nor Mike. However, the circumstances now were totally different. The streets and the City of Wilmington was once again safe, and the small talk of, "yeah they finally got his ass" and "I hope he gets the death penalty," could be heard by the Goods and the Cottmans who were seated together, and it ate at them to the core knowing they were referring to the man they all loved. To some of the victims' families who knew Tommy and Mike personally, they were shocked to even see the Goods and the Cottmans seated together due to the fact of the matter. But even under these conditions, neither family held a grudge because they all knew how close Mike and Tommy were. They were like brothers. The only thing that mattered to the Goods and the Cottmans now was the well-being of Mike's mental lapse and mind state, and Ann's freedom. She did not deserve to be held in a prison on the count of loving her husband and being tight lipped when it came to anything about what she knew of Tommy and Mike. They (the Feds) had on more than one occasion offered Ann her freedom over the last six months, but she wouldn't say a word. She would do life in jail on the strength of her loyalty to her wedding vows and love for her husband before she said something that would incriminate him. And although they played a three hour confession tape of her husband saying shit she knew nothing about and shit that had her looking at her husband in a new light because of all the murders he confessed to, she still wouldn't talk. She had no idea that the man she married was that much of a killer.

"Fuck freedom," she told herself over and over again, "especially if it's going to do more damage to my husband than he already did by making the tape," she spoke to herself again as she sat month after month awaiting this day. The day of the preliminary hearing in which the lawyer told her she'd be going home, and the day couldn't have come sooner. She was ready to get the fuck up out of there and home with her kids where she belonged. Jail was definitely not the look for her, she knew, and then she heard the Marshalls bringing another prisoner(s) down into the holding cells where she was awaiting her time to go to court. When the keys got louder and the footsteps sounded nearer, she sprung up off of the stainless steel slab used as a bench and ran over to the door to look out and be nosey, hopefully to see her husband, and then she screamed, "Hey babe!" but quickly cut it short because they were placing him in the cell across from her. There was no way in the world she wanted her outburst to cause her to lose her chance at seeing and being this close to her husband because the pussy ass C.O.s today could be some real 'dickheads' with the skin pulled back, especially if they knew it could annoy you. Had they heard her scream and put two and two together, she was sure they would have moved Mike to another cell just for spite, so she held her composure. She hadn't seen or talked to her husband in six whole months other than through letters and now she would have the chance as soon as these niggaz who must have failed the real cop test left.

■■■■■■

When the Marshalls led Mike down the hallways under the courtroom towards the cell blocks, he prayed he'd see his wife in one of the other lock-up cells. He needed to see her, know she was alright, and let her know himself that he and other things would be alright. So when he was led through the sliding doors towards the cell blocks and heard and seen her scream, "Hey babe!" he almost lost his composure, but quickly checked himself and shook his head "No" to her when he heard the Marshall say, "put him right here," because it was directly across the hall from her.

Mike couldn't wait until the Marshalls took the cuffs off of him so he could holla at his wife. Six months of not physically seeing her had him going crazy, not that he wasn't already, but seeing her, just looking into her eyes had restored what sanity he once had back to him because before this moment he was surely not all there. The rape and murder of his sister, Michelle and his own killing of his brother and other half had sent him into a serious mental lapse. It had taken him all the way back in his mind to the days of those long ass sessions at his psychiatrist's office he used to have as a child, and it's been that way since he swung that machete that took Tommy's head off. Every single day after that day at least one time a day, Mike wept mainly at night as he lay awake on his bunk in his cell while he cried himself to sleep. The only thing that would help him clear his mind was the voodoo and witchcraft books he read. This had nearly every other inmate on his tier afraid. No one wanted to do or say anything wrong to Mike Cottman, the man they heard so much about, even though they each held in questions they wanted to ask the man they admired which was easy to do. Being in jail for a while had a way of attracting those that were in for awhile to the inmates that just came in because they knew that they had fresh stories about the streets to tell. You know the who's who, what the bitches doing, and what niggaz is getting the money stories. And they all knew Mike had stories to tell. Shit, he was the largest nigga they knew. Yet they were still all afraid to ask him. They knew he was vicious and none of them wanted to chance being rooted so they let him be. Mike would lap the yard daily talking to himself outwardly and breaking into laughter at times while he walked, which had people wondering, wondering how this crazy mufucka was able to get all that money on the streets, but he had. However, money was the last thing on Mike's mind at this point. He was too guilt stricken and mentally unstable to focus on anything other than Tommy and what he had did to him. All he wanted to do now was join him in the afterlife and hoped like hell these crackers uptown in the suits, the ones who decided your fate, gave him the death penalty. All he wanted to do now was explain the way he was feeling and what he wanted to Ann. He knew that if there was anything or anyone in the world who would understand him, he knew it was Ann. The woman who had been with him since the summer of Tommy's block party when he turned twelve that Uncle Bear threw, up until now. The six months they have been incarcerated was the longest time they ever been apart or separate from one another, but that was over now. Mike was back with Ann even though they were in different cells, and he was sure that everything would be alright after they talked. So as soon as the Marshalls rounded the corner and they heard the door slid shut, they began.....

"Hey babe" Ann yelled through the door, "you alright?"

"Huh? I can't really hear you," Mike shot back.

"I said are you alright?" she yelled again, but again Mike couldn't hear her so he pointed down. Ann looked and smiled when she noticed the six inch gap under the doorway, then lay down on the concrete floor on her stomach. Mike did the same and just like magic they were eye to eye.

"Oh my God! Baby is you alright?" she said again and this time he heard her clearly.

"I am now," he responded with a huge smile, and Ann knew just by the smile it was one of relief. She knew her husband like the back of her hand and the smile on his face now was one with the equivalency of the one he had after he killed Deacon Johnson.

"Good. I am too," she let him know; being strong like she usually did at their weakest points. "I love you."

"Love you too," Mike said proudly to his wife. He admired everything about his wife, but her stomach was what he admired most. She was his backbone, the one who held him together when he would fall apart, and now even in a jail cell where he knew she was probably lost, she still stayed strong.

"How have you been? Have you been taking your medicine?" she asked concerned because she knew that they did help him stay level.

"Yeah I been taking my medicine mom," he joked. "Are you alright?"

"Yeah I'm good. I'm more worried about you than anything else baby. What we going to do?"

Mike hesitated at that question because he didn't know where to begin. There just wasn't any kind of way to tell your wife that you were ready to die. Better yet, tell her you were going to ask to die. It didn't sound right to Mike as he thought about it, so he imagined how it would sound rolling off his tongue. This was a time in which he knew he had to choose his words wisely.

"So what are we going to do?" Ann asked him impatiently. She wanted an answer; actually the way she asked him demanded an answer, and rightfully so, she was playing on the same team. Hell, she was the starting quarterback.

They way Mike was hesitating right now, Ann knew he was caught up on deciding whether or not he should be truthful or not. Lord knows this was the messiest situation that they ever been in, but he hadn't been dishonest with her before, "so why start now?" she was thinking as she waited on his answer.

"So?" she asked again.

"Ann baby," Mike began, "I fucked up. I fucked up bad. Baby I dug a hole I can't get out of."

"What do you mean?" she asked, but knew all too well what he was talking about.

"I mean, I told these mufuckas everything, everything babe. I told them mufuckas shit they didn't even know about."

"Why?"

"Because that's how I felt. I knew that if I told these mufuckas everything that I'd get the death penalty."

"The death penalty?"

"Yeah, the death penalty."

"Why? Why would you want them to give you the death penalty?"

"Because I don't deserve to live baby."

"What?! Boy you talking stupid right now."

"No I'm not. I'm serious baby. What da fuck I gotta live for, huh? I killed my brother," Mike said beginning to get choked up. "I killed my mufuckin brother," he said more emotional now.

"Baby stop. Stop doing that to yourself. You're killing yourself right now. Mike it was an accident."

"Accident or not baby, Tommy is gone. I killed him baby," Mike cried.

"Babe don't. Don't cry baby, you're about to make me cry," Ann told him because it was almost unbearable to see him crying. Mike was her rock and to see him cry brought her to the undeniable truth of what kind of trouble her husband was really in. There was a real chance that Mike could get the death penalty and the thought of it made her insides cry. On the outside though, she knew she had to stay strong, strong for her husband's sake. Strong like the day he put that eyeball in her hand. The eyeball she later came to know of it being the Deacon's. "Baby everything is going to be alright."

"How?"

"How? Because we're going to make it alright?"

"Baby it'll never be alright again. I'm ready to die," he continued to tear.

"Die?"

"Yeah die because I'll be damned if I want to spend the rest of my life in this mufucka," he said, and Ann understood him.

Dying in jail was something no one wanted to do, so in that sense she could relate. However, when it came to her, she was selfish. She couldn't imagine him dead. Not being able to see or talk to him would drive her crazy, so she thought real optimistically before saying; "Baby there's always a chance that your case could get overturned or something."

"Come on now baby, think about what you're saying. I gave them mufuckas a three hour confession tape. Once the jury and courtroom hear that tape, I'm done. And ain't no judge in the world going to overturn my case. When these mufuckas give me life or the death penalty, that's what I got, and if I had a choice I'd rather be dead," he said as he watched Ann's eyes start to water. "I'm sorry babe that's just how I feel."

Hearing those words roll off of his tongue and listening to the sincerity in his voice had finally cracked Ann's shell. What he was saying was the truth, but she wasn't going to allow him to see her physically cry. She was his backbone and she knew it and no matter how bad she wanted to let it out, she couldn't for Mike's sake.

"I see babe," she said and truly felt what he was saying.

"Do you?"

"Yes I do. I wouldn't want to spend the rest of my life in here either," Ann agreed but didn't want to sound too hard because there was a great chance that this was going to be his reality. So instead she spoke the words with understatement. "Yes I do," she repeated and for the rest of their time there until the Marshalls came back to take them upstairs into the courtroom, they made small talk and enjoyed a few laughs.

■■■■■■

"Cottman! Mike Cottman!" the first Marshall, a male officer yelled as he entered the cell block.

"Cottman! Ann Cottman!" a female officer followed suit as they approached their holding cells, "time for court."

Mike and Ann were led through the hallways beneath the federal courthouse towards the elevator. As they walked side by side, chained, cuffed, and shackled, all Mike thought was, "Damn my baby is a soldier," while Ann was thinking back on her wedding day when they stood side by side at the altar, was thinking about the birth of their first child, thinking back on the days when doctors labeled her husband crazy, thinking about how she went against everyone and followed her heart by staying with the only love she ever knew. The love that she wished everyone had an opportunity to experience. She was also thinking about court, then the outcome. She wanted to again drop some tears, but she knew she couldn't, not now anyway. Instead, when they reached the elevator she leaned forward to kiss him despite being told by the Marshalls not to talk and Mike did the same. Knowing the severity of both their cases because it was a media headline, the Marshalls allowed them their moment together because they knew it would be the last time they ever had the chance.

"I love you Mike Cottman," Ann spoke now dying instead of crying on the inside.

"I love you too Ann Cottman," Mike shot back instantly flipping into that villain society knew him as. Ann smiled; she noticed the ego state he flipped into. "My baby," she thought then thanked the Marshalls.

"You're welcome," the Marshalls said in unison.

Inside the courtroom, the couple was led before the judge and seated at the defense table. They heard their children yell out, "Hi mommy!! Hi daddy!!" and it caused the courtroom to chuckle. The ones who didn't see it as funny felt sad, and a few, "That's a shame," and "Awes," could be heard. For Mike and Ann the feelings were mixed. For the next two and a half hours and two recesses, the United States Government vs. The Cottmans preliminary came to a close. The evidence revealed was overwhelmingly not good for Mike at all. Nonetheless, the evidence that they had against Ann was absolutely meaningless. And just like her lawyer told her, Ann was going home. Mike's trial date was scheduled for next summer, and the court was adjourned.

Chapter Nineteen

Today was the day that marked the celebration of their six months being together as a couple, and it was also her birthday. Her life had totally done a three hundred sixty degree turn around from where she was just a little over a year ago when her dream life went from sugar to shit at the very hands of the man she loved and was in love with since the day she laid eyes on him. However, when she found her all white teddy bear that was taken from her on Christmas day, along with her parents at his sister Brooklyn's house, she was never the same and thought that she'd never be capable of loving again. That was until she met him. The man who helped her restore her life and things couldn't have been going more smoothly than they were right now. Their relationship and what they had together was what the author, Danielle Steele could have easily turned into a New York bestselling novel with nearly no effort at all. The chemistry the two of them had together was unmistakably the work of Allah (God), and everyone that came in contact with them wanted what they had. Their shit was special. But like always, in every scenario where there was a "Pro" along came a "Con". Misery loves company, so there came the gossip and people took it and ran with it like a sprinter being handed a baton in a relay race. It's fucked up that shit has to be that way, but people just can't stand to see something so positive happening in a place where anything good just wasn't supposed to be taking place. And we all know where that's at right? That's right, you guessed it; in a Black community! Society just had it designed that way. Designed for us to fail and keep us in a negative state of mind, which usually is miserable and depressed and the way they did it was by neglecting our needs. The little shit, like pot holes in the street unattended to. Abandoned houses that painted our communities to be eye-soaring to us, which kept our minds handcuffed into believing that this is all life has to offer us. So to help us self-destruct, to put the blame on us, to keep them in the clear, they put liquor stores on nearly every corner, and flooded the "Hood" with narcotics, which ultimately makes us commit unconscious suicide on ourselves, and the gossip that was being spread had her mind going crazy. Crazy with thoughts of a past she tried so hard to forget. Had her playing the scenes of a past that only she and Kiesha knew about and trying to remember if she had left anything behind that could link her to what happened back then just in case she became a suspect. And she was grateful that Madina had put her "D" on what people were saying in their gossip.

Madina was her hairdresser and nearly everyone else's hairdresser in the City of Wilmington and New Castle. So as a birthday gift to her girl Tamira, she came to her house and did her hair there. A very nice gift I may add, especially since her color was fading out, and she was in need of a "New Do" and perm. Plus, she was tired of rockin' the ponytail look, but hey she was who she was, one of the baddest bitches around hands muthafuckin' down.

"So what they saying Madina?" Tamira asked her while Madina held her head under the sink rinsing her.

"Guuurl, them muthafuckaz is saying all kinds of shit. They really think you had something to do with Greeny, Snotty, and Kyle's death," Madina told her, and then continued, "Gurl that is crazy as shit."

"Madina girl now you know that's some bullshit right?" Tamira asked her.

"Yeah gurl, you know I know its bullshit," Madina lied. She thought Tamira had something to do with it too, or at least knew some shit because Tamira did move on a little too fast for someone that just lost a child and a child's father. So in that aspect Madina did wonder.

"Well why you think they're saying it?"

"Probably because you moved on and jumped right back into a relationship so fast," she told her what she was thinking herself. "You feel me though? I mean just a little over a year ago you was burying your son and his father, now you talking about getting married and to Jaquan at that," Madina finished telling her what she thought about it all, and then led her over to the hair dryer with her head wrapped up in a towel.

"So what? What that mean?"

"Hold up now. Don't go there with me," Madina checked her feeling like the conversation was heading somewhere else.

Somewhere it didn't need to be going...

"Nah I ain't mean it like dat. I'm just saying: what dat mean? I moved on and got in a relationship because it just happened that way. Who da fuck wants to stay stuck back there wallowing in that shit. Fuck dat, not me. I didn't even expect it to go this far myself, it just happened that way feel me? I know what the real problem is, bitches is hating dat's all. Hating because I got Jaquan," Tamira stated matter-of-factly.

"Humph, you might be right gurl. You know what I say though, right?"

"What?"

"Do you gurl, do you," Madina told her. She ain't care one way or the other. Shit, her man just came home from a bid, and she was still in la-la land.

"Oh believe me Madina, I am girl."

"Right though."

"Imma do me and my baby Jaquan, you heard," Tamira said and their conversation switched to something else. Tamira was only half attentive though. Her mind was too busy remembering murder scenes and having flashbacks of episodes of forensic files. "Damn! I hope I don't become a suspect."

That was hours ago. Hours before now as she stood in front of her full length mirror naked, lotioning her body up with Victoria's Secret pear and cucumber body lotion. And no matter how bad she tried to forget about the things Madina said to her and focus on her day, her birthday, the one she was going to spend with Jaquan, she couldn't. It was just too much. Their talk had awakened her conscience. A conscience she tried to keep closed. The few stretch marks on her stomach from childbirth didn't help either. They made her feel guilty, guilty that she had murdered her own child, but she had to. There was no way that she could have gone on with her life looking at her son, the son that resembled her parents' killer so much. Having the baby around would have been the ultimate betrayal to her parents because he would have been a constant reminder, a reminder to her that she had made love and given birth for their killer. "Hell no!" she thought. To her that would have been like keeping a baby as a result of a rape. "Yeah right, not me!" Tamira said to herself and as quickly as she said it, she erased it from her mind. Today was her birthday and she was going to enjoy it. She refused to have her day ruined by thoughts of a past that she buried with her son and her son's father. So as she slid into her dress by "Gucci" and slipped on her heels to match and then threw the shoulder bag over her shoulder, she headed down the stairs to the door to answer the doorbell. Just like always, Jaquan was right on time.

"Hey baby!" she said when she opened the door and was greeted with a box and a handful of balloons.

"Hey baby, happy birthday," Jaquan answered. "You ready?"

"Yeah I'm ready. Just let me go put this stuff up right quick," she said then asked, "What's in the box?"

"Open it up and find out."

The box Tamira held in her hand was the size of a box that could possibly hold a sweater, so her mind was thinking clothing. She was anxious to see what the box contained, hoping it was that pair of "Seven" jeans she wanted, so she tore it open. To her surprise there was another box. Puzzled she gave him a crazy look like, "What's dis?" and he just smiled. So she continued on with the tirade of opening the gift. She tore the next one, and the next one, and the next one until there was a box the size of a ring and the tears started. "Oh my God, Jaquan! What's this?!"

"Just open it and find out," he told her.

When she opened up the last box, she was speechless. The size of the ring that sat on the black velour canvas took her breath away. It had to be at least three to four carats and seemed to be flawless, probably "VVS1" in clarity. For what seemed to be an eternity, she stood in complete silence from the shock and sight of the ring. She didn't speak another word until the silence was broken by Jaquan with the words, "Tamira baby, will you be my wife?"

"Oh my God, yes baby! Yes! I'll be your wife!" and she ran full speed into his arms and showered him with the most compassionate kiss she ever gave a person. This kiss had beat out her first kiss. The kiss with Jay Bird only days before he took her virginity at that base house on 23rd Street he used to hustle out of. The kiss people told her only happened once in a lifetime.

"Thank you baby, thank you," he told her when the kiss ended.

Jaquan had a full day of wonderful things to do with your mate. First they were going to have a nice lunch at a spot he found on 11th Street called "Pure Bred", then they were going to Baltimore to walk its Harbor and see the aquarium. Next he had planned for the two of them to see a play called "Why Men Cheat". Then they would top the night off with a Seafood dinner overlooking the Harbor's water. Lastly, they would cap it all off with some extensive love making. That was the plan, but shit never works out as planned. All that was interrupted by a phone call; the phone call from Detective Cohen letting him know that his uncle Pretty E was in custody, but in a state of delirium and couldn't make the phone call himself; couldn't make the call because he had been admitted to the State Hospital for the criminally insane. Jaquan couldn't believe it. He could not believe what the Detective was telling him. He couldn't believe his uncle had snapped and lost his mind, either that, or he just didn't want to accept the fact that his uncle had went crazy. Jaquan looked to Tamira and she just felt that something was wrong. His facial expression told her so.

"What baby? What's wrong?" she asked him.

"I'm sorry baby, but we have to cancel our plans," he began and finished telling her all that was just revealed to him. She looked at him and said, "Baby no need to be sorry, handle your business," and to lighten things up she added, "Nothing can spoil my day," and looked down at the huge ring on her left hand.

"Just know you gotta make it up to me, you hear?"

"You got dat baby."

"Ok just as long as you know," she replied with a grin, and Jaquan was out the front door headed to the police station.

■■■■■■

Pretty E was taken to the Wilmington Police Department, booked, fingerprinted, and charged with 1st degree murder and weapons charges. When that was all done and he sat for nearly twelve hours, he was transferred over to the State Hospital for the insane and placed on a criminal ward. It was the only option Detective Cohen had, even though he wanted him buried under one of those concrete steel jail cells. He figured that out the moment he read him his rights upon arresting him. Pretty E was not there at all and incoherent to every question that was asked of him, even hours later. He could not respond to any of the questions asked to him because he was too busy staring off into space or laughing and crying at the fact that his mental had cracked, and he was no longer in control of his mind. And although he was aware of his laughs and tears that fell from his eyes, there was nothing he could do to control it. He had lost his power and his tears for Egypt were now mixed with tears of his own; tears of frustration and the fact that he could not make his mind stop having these crazy thoughts. He would have never thought in all the days of his life that he would end up where he was now, butt naked in a paper gown and a padded room from the ceiling to the floor. Then he burst out into another huge laugh because the thought of it was funny as hell. "Damn I'm really butt butterball naked, huh?" he asked himself.

"You think you ain't?" he answered and burst out laughing again.

"Man you crazy as a muthafucka," he told himself and realized for the first time that he was talking out loud.

Chapter Twenty

This was not the same house that Ann remembered having before going to jail six months ago. Everything about it was different from the foyer to the rooms, to the windows to the driveway. It was completely made over thanks to Raven and her insurance company's contractors that had restored and remodeled the skeletal remains of the house she watched go up in flames as she drove away from a blood massacre and five alarm arson that she committed. The only thing that was the same about the house was the address, but she was grateful. The house was beautiful! Raven had done her thing decorating, from the paint to the "retro" furniture, and the house itself looked way better than when she and Mike first bought the house themselves. The equity even went up nearly a whole hundred thousand dollars more than the half a mil it was originally worth. The best thing about it all was that it was like the real "Heaven" in the sky compared to the cell she lived in for a half of a year.

Ann was grateful and overwhelmed with joy at the fact of being home, free, and reunited with her children. The only thing that took some major adjustments and getting used to was the fact that Mike wasn't there with her, and it was a strong possibility that he would never be there again. A hard pill to swallow especially when Ann hadn't been apart from Mike, her husband since the days of 'boys chase the girls' and 'hide and go get it' when they were kids. Just knowing that in itself was enough to break Ann down. And that first night home, after she put the kids to bed, she broke and released what she had bottled up inside of her for years. All the pain she held for Mike and his situation, the pain she felt for her sons having to grow up fatherless, and mainly all the shit she held in for herself had finally released. That night, Ann must've had let out two gallons of tears from each eye as she wept for hours. When she was done, she felt a relief so satisfying she almost felt like herself, but she'd never feel that way again, at least not until she found out what was going to happen to Mike. Only then would she be able to put her mind at ease. Then, just like always Ann snapped back into the strong black woman she was. She had to if not for herself, at least for the kids and Mike's sake, and nothing was going to stop her from being just that, her husband's "Super Woman".

The next morning Ann was awakened by the doorbell and a knock on her front door. Not to mention the crying of her youngest son who she knew by the way he wailed, that her oldest son was punching on him again. It was just that mother's intuition.

"Boy what I tell you about that shit?! Do you want your ass beat? Huh? What I tell you about hitting on him? That's your little brother! Hit them boys in the street like that," she snapped and when she got up on him, he ran.

"I ain't chasing you, but you believe when I catch you I'm a tear dat ass up! Watch!" she promised him, and then went to answer the person at the door; standing on the other side was a person she came to know and love like a little sister, Raven. She was on the other side and boy did she need somebody to talk to, well listen to her at least because she sure had a lot to tell her. Maybe she could get some advice from her. Some ways on how to deal with weight of the world that now rested on her shoulders. If not, she'd at least be able to get it off her chest.

"Girl you don't know how glad I am to see you," Ann said when she opened the door. "I'm stressed da fuck out!"

"I bet, but you need to know that your lil sis is here for you, you hear?" Raven replied.

"Thanks girl. Come on in and sit down!"

Raven took Tommy Jr.'s Polo hat off when they entered the house, and he ran straight in the den to play with his cousins, while the two of them, Ann and Raven took their seats in the living room to talk. To have the talk she so desperately needed. "Girl I don't even know where to begin?" Ann started off then went straight into her stay at prison. Over the next hour and a half or so, Ann told her everything she was going through. When she was done "Damn!" was all Raven could say.

"Girl that was almost too much to digest," Raven said.

"Tell me about it. Imagine having to go through it."

"So he actually told you he wanted the death penalty?"

"Yeah he told me that girl, to my face, but now that I actually had a chance to think about it, I can't blame him. Can you imagine spending the rest of your life in jail?"

"I can't imagine a day."

"So on that note, do you blame him? I just can't picture him not being here no more. If they do give him the death penalty," she paused holding back the need to cry, "girl it's going to be like I died," Ann told her and just the mere thought of them killing her husband was too much to bare. The tears were about to start again.

Let it out sis. Let them mufuckin tears out. That shit ain't doing you no good being held in. Letting it out can't do nuffin but help. That shit'll make you feel better," Raven told her and gave her a hug. When she did, the tears fell like rain. It was probably from the hug Raven gave her. The comfort of just being held, cradled, and knowing someone was there with you, that you weren't alone, whatever it was, it sure felt good to have a shoulder to lean on.

"That's right big sis, let it go! Lord knows I cried a many of nights when Tommy first died.

For the rest of the day Raven never left her side. They were conjoined at the hip with the kids in tow as they shared an entire day together. A day of just them and the kids doing shit together lost in the time they had free of the worries that lied at home as they roamed the Christiana Mall shopping. It was definitely what the doctor ordered for them and the kids. They enjoyed themselves more than they did, as they skipped behind their mothers' with arms full of toys.

The more the day went on, the better Ann began to feel. The entire day of shopping, eating fatty foods like McDonald's which she never eats, and walking had worn her out. Raven shot a movie suggestion out there to Ann and she bit on it so they let the kids pick a movie. They ended up going to see a movie called "The Princess and The Frog" which was actually good then they headed home. Raven decided to stay all night which Tommy loved. And like a real sister, Raven slept at Ann's side. Tonight, just for tonight, Ann was not alone in bed.

∎∎∎∎∎∎

The day Ann had marked off on her calendar; the one she couldn't wait to come had finally come. It was that time; the time to go to court for trial, and now she didn't want to go. She was too scared to learn the outcome of her husband's fate. There was a real strong possibility that he'd lose trial and get the death penalty, but there was still that little glimmer of hope that what the lawyer told her would work. They were going to base their whole defense on his mental diagnosis and the fact that he was legally insane. That was the only way to defend a client that had already admitted his guilt. They just hoped that they could pursue the jury to see it that way. If not, at least one because then they'd get a hung jury which would be like a win for them. They'd be happy with any verdict other than a "Guilty" one. So after she stood from her knees from praying, she grabbed her car keys and headed to the courthouse on King St.

∎∎∎∎∎∎

"Cottman! Cottman!" the C.O. called out to him through the intercom system into his cell. "Cottman!" he called out again just a little bit louder this time.

"Huh? Yeah what's up?" Mike answered groggily and upset. Mad that he had been awakened out of his sleep from the dream he was having. The one about him and his wife, Ann making love on their king sized luxury firm Stearns & Foster mattress. "Shit!" he cursed.

"Cottman you have court today. You need to start getting ready ok?" the C.O. told him.

"Alright I'm up! I'll be ready when you crack the door," Mike told the guard, but lay on his bunk a little while longer. Today was the day his trial began on murder charges, and it was taking him some time to motivate himself to get up. It would take anybody some time to get motivated under these circumstances, especially since it wasn't going to be that much of a trial. Shit, he already admitted to everything he was being charged with. However, there was still that little glimmer of hope his wife, Ann and Mike's defense team held for a different outcome. An outcome other than a "Guilty" verdict, one that surely held the death penalty on just the decapitation of Tommy Good alone, let alone the bodies of Zy, Boomer, and Peacock he led them to. They were stuck on and hoping for an insanity verdict, which would bring about an entirely different outcome. And from his past history alone, Mike was a shoe-in candidate for that type of verdict, which would be a win for them. A win because Mike would be spared his life and probably be placed in a psychiatric ward at the State Hospital for the criminally insane; a far cry away from a prison cell. A cell that usually held you and two other muthafuckas with one on the floor due to an overcrowded population of inmates, with a sink, toilet, and two inch thick mattress. Not to mention the constant clatter of keys and the window view of a huge steel gate surrounded with barbwire and razor wire. Prison alone was enough to crack the most stable mind, so imagine what it would to one that was already lost? That's why Mike's defense team was fighting so hard for him. That and the bonus one hundred thousand Ann promised them. Anything other than the State Hospital for the insane would be a loss because unlike prison, the hospital was something like freedom.

At the hospital, Ann would be allowed six to eight hour visits on the weekend outside on their campus-like yard where the patients grew vegetables and flowers unsupervised. Mike would still have his life and a home-like living arrangement with the possibility of being released back into society if the doctors deemed him appropriate. What more can one ask for, especially one who made a three hour confession tape to all kinds of shit. It was a long shot, but it sure was feasible, especially since the State of Delaware labeled him legally insane, "manic depressive", a long time ago.

"Cottman! It's that time. You ready?" the C.O. asked.

"Yeah I'm ready. Pop the door," Mike answered.

Outside of his cell on the tier, Mike took a seat at one of the steel tables with another inmate who had court this morning. Both of them were so deep in thought about the matter at hand that they didn't speak to one another. They just acknowledged each other with a head nod. Before long, they were being led out into the hallway and escorted down to booking and receiving to be counted and logged out for court.

Once down in booking and receiving, Mike was led into the bullpen where about thirty other inmates waiting for court were at. "Damn I hate this shit," he thought to himself as he maneuvered his way through them to catch a seat on the steel bench. This was the only part about going to court that everybody hated. They hated it mainly because it was only four something in the morning and court didn't start until nine. Then on top of all of that, they crammed you up in a little holding cell with one toilet that everybody had to use without an ounce of privacy. And to make it all worse, you had to sit there and listen to a whole bunch of bullshit war stories so when Mike saw

"Hard Rock", an old junkie from off of Bennett St. he was glad he had someone to talk to.

"Hard Rock!" What's up nigga?" Mike yelled across the holding cell overtop of the chitter chatter of the other inmates.

"Oh shit! If it ain't dat nigga killer Mike? What's up youngster? You ok?" Hard Rock, the junkie who knew him and Tommy from the days when Uncle Bear was around, asked.

"Yeah I'm good. Good as it's going to be you dig?"

"Yeah I can dig that."

"So what's going on out there?" Mike asked the ol' head.

"Awe man a whole lot of nuffin. Niggaz ain't been holding it down since you left. Bennett St. is fucked up. The only nigga out there now that's holding it down is the nigga Jaquan. Speaking of him, did you hear about his Uncle Pretty E? Man, that nigga done snapped out and killed the bitch Tammy. They got him chained up in a straight jacket somewhere down the State Hospital."

"Oh yeah?"

"Hell yeah."

"What? The nigga went crazy or something?"

"Man that nigga fucked up from what I hear. Talking to himself and all kinds of shit," Hard Rock told him, then said, "enough about that, what's up wit 'chu?" he asked wanting to be nosey.

"Man it's hard to tell right now," Mike said and leaned in close to Hard Rock before saying, "we going after an insanity verdict you dig? You know them muthafuckas already got me labeled insane. So I should be good," Mike finished then it all started to make sense.

"Oh I see," Hard Rock said then continued, "good luck," and stood to walk away because the guards were calling off names now. "Man that nigga ain't got it all," Hard Rock said to himself then glanced over his shoulder at Mike. What he saw in his eyes was the same thing he saw the night of Deacon Johnson's murder, a crazed man and the reason why that memory stuck out the most to Hard Rock was because he had just taken a hit. He was sure that if Mike knew he was there that night that he'd been buried right next to the deacon.

Chapter Twenty-One

Pretty E had been so heavily sedated with medications when he was first brought in that now as he was awakened from his sleep, he hadn't the slightest idea of where he was at. His head felt heavy and his mind was drawing a blank right now. The only thing that was making some kind of sense was the lady on the loud system letting everyone know that dinner was being served in the mess hall. That made a whole lot of sense because his stomach was growling and the only thing that could settle it was a nice plate of hot food. "But where am I at?" he asked himself. Then slowly the more he thought about what he just asked himself, the more he remembered. He remembered being arrested, he remembered a little bit about what happened to Tammy, and he remembered that he needed to call Egypt. That's where the insanity began for him. His mind just couldn't conceive the fact that Egypt had been murdered and was no longer around.

Pretty E got out of his bed and headed for the door to the room he was in. When he reached it, he turned the knob and looked out. What he saw was men in blue scrubs like the ones he had on, and women in pink ones all headed in the same direction so he stepped out. For a minute he thought he was in detox but Ms. Ruth wasn't there to take his vital signs, and the floor was carpeted instead of buffed and waxed. The hallway was also furnished in an upscale type of manner and painted in smooth and relaxing colors so he knew he wasn't in prison. It wasn't until he saw some nurses and orderlies that he figured out he was in some sort of hospital, and then as he stopped at the nurses' station to ask for a phone call, he knew just what kind of hospital he was in. The State Hospital for the insane and what verified it was a woman named Leslie that he'd soon come to know. She was down in a squatting position making kissing noises and saying, "Here kitty, kitty."

"Come on now Leslie," an orderly interrupted her. "Time to eat."

"I know but kitty has to eat too."

"I already fed kitty," the orderly said then she allowed him to escort her away, but Pretty E didn't see a kitty.

"Hi Mr. Williams, I see you finally woke up. How do you feel? And what would you like me to call you, Eric or Mr. Williams?" the nurse at the station asked him.

"Eric is fine," Pretty E told her then nearly jumped out his skin as a man ran past him screaming like a Nascar engine.

"Sccccccuuuuuurrrr!!! Rumph! Rumph!" he yelled as he revved up his imaginary engine and raced past Pretty E and the nurses' station.

"Mr. Martin stop that! No running!" the nurse yelled out to him and his run turned into a fast walk. She giggled but mainly at the way Eric had jumped. "Don't mind Mr. Martin. He used to have dreams of winning the Dover Downs Monster Mile.

"Damn that's fucked up. He crazy as a muthafucka," Pretty E said to the nurse who gave him a: "Uh hello and you're not?" type of look.

"No Eric, Mr. Martin and Leslie are not crazy. Crazy is a bad word like all that cursing you're doing."

"My bad," he cut in.

"Good," she replied then continued, "let's just say that Mr. Martin and Leslie, and everyone else in here is just misunderstood. Ok?"

"Ok," Pretty E replied. "But can I make a phone call now?"

"After dinner I'll let you make a call ok?"

"Ok," Pretty E said and walked in the direction of the smell of the food and the way the patients went.

Pretty E was more confused now than anything. His mind was in between sanity and insanity, but for the most part he had it under control. Something he hadn't had in a long time. That was all soon to change though. The way his brain worked now, after he snapped out like he did, it only allowed him to maintain sanity for streaks and moments at a time. So when he walked into the mess hall and saw the other patients and their behaviors, he automatically clicked in. Pretty E went from medium to an extreme low in seconds. That's how manic depressants are. Before he realized what he was doing, he was chewing up his coffee instead of sipping it. That's right; coffee, sugar, and creamer, no water. Pretty E was misunderstood too.

After dinner, the patients were led out the side door of the mess hall into a smoking quarters and the yard for recreation. Pretty E was still carrying his cup. His little Styrofoam cup hat would become his trademark, as he walked over to a bench and took a seat under the shaded tree. Battling with the voices in his head and trying to understand them, only made him more mental. His medical diagnosis as of now was schizophrenic (multiple personalities) and incompetent to stand trial. The murder charges against him would have to wait; a good thing because now he probably wouldn't do a day in jail. As for now, he just laughed and cried, cried and laughed and enjoyed the natural high his brain was giving him. It felt like to him that the world had slipped him a "Mickey". Pretty E would never be the same.

■■■■■■

There were two guards, one on each side of him as he was led from the holding cell behind the courtroom where his trial was to begin, to the doors that led to it. Once they were just beyond the doors of the courtroom, they uncuffed him leaving him in only leg irons, and then escorted him in. No sooner than Mike stepped foot in the courtroom, he heard a loud outburst of a woman crying. By the way she wailed, he knew it was one of his victims' loved ones. Just hearing her agony caused a smile to form on each corner of his lips. Then he heard the cameras snapping; only there weren't any flashes due to the rules of the courthouse, but the press was still in full stride. As Mike was led across the courtroom, his smile grew wider with each step closer to the defense table, because he began noticing his loved ones. The sight of Ann, Raven, Big Mom, and all of Tommy's cousins he grew up with, put him in a good mood. Even cool ass Dave, the state trooper, was in attendance only he was in plain clothes. They smiled back, but had been fore-warned by the bailiff before he was led in that if they tried to communicate with him, they would be led out of the courtroom one by one. So to acknowledge that they noticed Mike, they all shot up a quick wave and head nod. He nodded back, and then was seated. This was on day one of the trial.

Over the next week and a half of trial, there would be more outbursts and sobs from the victims' families. Even Mike's people cringed as the prosecution team presented their case in the form of a slide show on the projector of the loved ones family members' at their times of death. The sights and scenes were so eerie and grotesque that most people in the courtroom couldn't stomach it. What the most horrific thing about it was though, was the fact that Mike, in his heavily accented deep Southern voice had narrated the slide show. It was part of his three hour confession tape he made at the station. By the time the prosecution presented its case to the jurors, there wasn't a single person present that could think of anything other than a "Guilty" verdict.

"Prosecution rests," the lead prosecutor, Mark Weneagar said.

"Defense," the Honorable Judge Livingsworth said.

"Yes your Honor," Chuck O'Berly began his defense. Over the next three days doctor after doctor and expert after expert took the stand in Mike's defense. By each one of them being a specialist in their field, it was mandatory that the jurors took into consideration what they were presenting to them about Mike and a person with his diagnosis. What they were all explaining was that a person legally insane could not be accountable for what his mind caused him to do. It could have been a mental lapse or a side effect from one of the many psych meds he was on. Whatever the case, the State of Delaware knew that this man was insane years ago, yet they still let him stay out in society.

"So I say to you, the people of the jury, blame the State's lead doctor for missing a judgment on my client's mental state, not my client for doing what one of his many personalities led him to do. I rest my case," the lawyer said, landing the most powerful blow of this trial.

"Anything further?" Judge Livingsworth asked.

"Nothing further," both sides agreed.

"I turn the case over to you, the jurors," the judge said and left the jury to deliberate.

For the next two days the jury deliberated over a verdict before finally coming up with one. The courtroom was so antsy that when they were led back into the jury box, everyone was on the edge of their seats anticipating the outcome.

"Has the jury reached a verdict?" Judge Livingsworth asked.

"Yes we have your Honor," the jury's foreman said as he stood to his feet. "We the jury find the defendant, Michael Cottman, innocent of first degree murder. However, we the jury do find the defendant guilty of second degree murder by reason of insanity. We believe that the defendant needs to be placed in the state's psychiatric ward in the State Hospital for the criminally insane to be evaluated by the medical staff there until they deem him appropriate or stable enough to return to society," he paused then finished with, "if ever, your Honor."

The jury's decision brought about a delayed reaction because it took some time to register. Mike's family applauded and cheered in victory on the defensive side of the courtroom, while the few males on the victims' side of the courtroom were outraged.

"That's some bullshit!!" one of them yelled and a small melee erupted as they began tossing chairs in Mike's direction. Mike smiled then pointed his finger in their direction in the manner of a gun and shouted, "Pow! Pow!" before breaking out into laughter as he was led from the courtroom. The trial was over, Ann had won. Her husband's life would be spared.

■■■■■■

A month and a half later, Mike was sentenced to the Asylum by Judge Livingsworth. And like always, to every "Pro" there was a "Con". In Mike's case, his was the obvious; the "Pro" was that he would be spared his life and duck a prison term, while his "Con" was that the court stipulated him to be "upped" in his dosage of medications. Instead of Seraquil and Trazodone, he was now forced to take Thorazine and "Hal-Dog", two of the strongest psych meds prescribed to man. When he refused because the medicine kept him cloudy, the prison's "Quick Response Team" would hold him down in his cell while the nurses injected him. That only made matters worse. See the medications Thorazine and "Hal-Dog" actually made you crazy and dependent on it to function normally. So by the time sentencing day came around, Ann and the rest of Mike's family barely recognized him. The medication had caused him to gain nearly thirty pounds. He had given up on his appearance so his hair was unkempt and full of prison blanket lint, and his eyes were distant. He also acquired a little twitch. That was Mike's "Con", if he wasn't crazy before, he was now, the medication made him that way. Ann cried at the sight of him.

The minute they brought Mike in she knew that something wasn't right. Mike almost looked like a zombie. The medication he was on had him fucked up to a point where he didn't even know what was going on. He was just there. But Ann, she knew that this was a possibility from all the research she had done on the two medications after the Judge ordered them. She just hoped and prayed that he would be head strong enough to maintain and function like he always did. She was so wrong and far away from the notion, that when he came in she broke down. She didn't expect things to be this bad, but she did suspect something because his phone calls stopped and she was denied visits because of his behavioral problems. Nonetheless, she still stayed optimistic, like now. Even though he strolled in zombie-like, she still had hope. After today, his prison stay would be over and he'd be transferred to the State Hospital for the criminally insane and the healing would begin. Soon, Ann would have her husband back, or so she thought.

■■■■■

Pretty E was sitting in the recreational room chewing up his coffee as usual while he watched an episode of "The Family Guy", the patients' favorite show. Months had passed, and he hadn't gotten any better at all. There were still times in which he would catch those little stints of normality and his mind would think rational, but that didn't last long because as quick as it came it went. Like now, his normal thoughts floated away as he thought for a moment, "Why ain't no water in my cup?" but he went right back to chewing anyway. Crazy was now his normal, and normal was his crazy. It had become so sad that Jaquan had fallen back from coming to see him all the time. He did constantly stay up on the doctors' and shit though. It was fucked up how the brain worked once you lost control of it. Then, out of nowhere the orderlies brought in a new patient to introduce to them all.

"Good evening everyone," the lead orderly said.

"Good evening Mr. Matthews!" they all chimed.

"I want everyone to say hello to Michael."

"Hello Michael!" they all greeted the new patient cheerfully, everyone except Pretty E.

Pretty E's mind was drawing a serious blank right now as he stared at the new patient named Mike. He didn't know why, but for some strange or odd reason he felt like he knew the guy from somewhere before. Maybe he was one of his associates from the past, could have been a friend, but Pretty E felt he must've been someone of importance to him because his vibe was too strong. He tried as hard as he could to remember the man before him and was making progress, that was until the frustration of not being able to remember set in and Pretty E gave up, gave in to one of the many voices that now lingered in his head and walked over to introduce himself.

Mike looked out over the recreational room for anything familiar. A person, a piece of furniture, a wall portrait, anything, and there was nothing. Nothing at all familiar about the place he now stood in that he remembered. There was something about the place he noticed was different from where he just left, and that was that there were no cops around. Instead, there were doctors and nurses, and orderlies who all treated him kind. None of them was harsh like the cops who used to beat him in his cell and force him to take medicine.

Medicine that deep down inside, he knew was the reason why he felt like he did. Like the world was moving in slow motion, at a snail's pace, and he couldn't remember a thing that happened longer than a few hours ago, a fucked up feeling for someone who used to be so sharp mentally. A person who had fooled psychiatrists and doctors into believing he was crazy after the death of his twin sister, Michelle. Mike had fooled everyone, everyone except Ann who stood by his side despite everything that was being said in the beginning. Now, as a result of beating the system, the system had come back to beat him. The system had took his sanity and locked it somewhere deep within him with the keys called Thorazine and "Hal-Dog". I guess the sayings are true, "What goes around comes around" and "Sometimes you get the bear and sometimes the bear gets you". Whatever the case may be, Mike was on the receiving end of some shit called Karma.

Tired of standing in the same spot he was in since being introduced to his new friends and fellow patients, he moved across the "Rec" room to grab a seat on an empty sofa. Mike sat back on the soft cushions of the couch, leaned his head back on the back of it, and then let his eyes rest for a moment. He let them remain closed for a few minutes while he listened to the sounds and people around him. Some talked to themselves, some talked to imaginary friends, and some even had imaginary pets, cars, and bicycles. The shit going on around him was so crazy he started to silently wish he had an imaginary friend or something himself. That's when he felt the tap on his leg and looked to see some dude standing before him.

"Hi I'm Eric," Pretty E said.

"Hi Eric, I'm Mike," Mike responded and the two of them shook hands, and then stared into each other's eyes. For a moment it actually seemed like they remembered one another from somewhere before, they just couldn't put a finger on it. Nevertheless, from that day on they had become the best of friends.

"Hollywood Caliber Books That Should Be Movies!!!"

Epilogue

Its funny how days, weeks, months, and years pass by without the slightest inclination that it's going by so fast without you noticing it, that is, until you look up in the mirror and the reflection of the face you knew to once be so youthful now has creases in it and a receding hairline. Maybe even having a few teeth fall out. Whatever the reason may be, that's when you begin to look back and try and see if you have done all that you could have done in your lifetime. No one wants to be the person that should've, could've, or would've. You only have one life to live, so why not live it like there's no fucking tomorrow?! That's how Pretty E and Mike lived their lives clean up until their lifestyle ultimately landed them here together. Together at the State Hospital in a ward for the criminally insane where they became best friends, even now twenty years later.

So now, as they sat at the chess table under their favorite shaded tree playing their one billionth game of chess at fifty years old for Mike and nearly sixty for Pretty E, they now favored Martin Lawrence and Eddie Murphy in the movie "Life". Their once wavy, sharply cut temple tapers were now salt and pepper gray baby afros. Their once used to be perfect smiles now had been replaced with dentures due to the medication rotting their teeth out, and their once tall, firm, and erect body postures were now leaning slightly forward and canes were used to keep them erect now. The medicine had eaten away at their calcium level to a point that their bone marrow was fragile. Yet, through all of that, there were still times in which they caught glimmers of past memories of life when they were normal. Short flashbacks of sane times and right now it was happening to Pretty E.

"Come on man! Are you going to move your piece or not?" Pretty E asked Mike.

"Yeah Imma move it when I get ready nigga!" Mike shot back angrily. And no sooner than the word nigga rolled off his tongue, it all came back to Pretty E. This muthafucka across from him was Mike Cottman, Tommy Good's right hand man. The nigga who shot up Dog's funeral, killed Rasul, Egypt, and Davita, and he was sitting across from him like nothing ever happened.

"Ain't this a bitch?!" Pretty E shouted and stood to his feet clutching his cane tightly.

"What?" Mike asked clueless.

"This," Pretty E said and raised his cane high above his head. "Smack!" the cane sounded as it found its resting place on the top of Mike's head. "Smack!" it landed again. It was the second one that jarred Mike's memory back, but it was too late. Pretty E was all over him and beating him to death.

By the time the orderlies came to restrain him it was a lost cause. Mike had been beaten to death and was lying in a pool of blood, and Pretty E was being taken away to the padded room and placed in a straight jacket. That night, at the top of his lungs he yelled, "I got him back y'all!" talking to Dog, Davita, Rasul, and Egypt then laughed himself to sleep.

■■■■■■

Months later when Pretty E was allowed back into population, everyone noticed he wasn't the same. It was like he was in a deep depression of some sort; maybe mourning the death of his friend Mike. So as he passed the nurses' station, one of them asked, "Eric what's wrong? Why such the long face?"

"My dick died," he responded.

Shocked, the nurse left it alone. Three days later, Pretty E walked by the same nurse station only this time he was naked.

"Eric why are you naked?" the same nurse asked.

"Because today is the viewing," Pretty E said.

That's right you guessed it. Pretty E was still crazy as a bedbug.

COMING SOON

Happy F$ckin' New Year!
"Brooklyn's Revenge"

Chapter One

The snow was falling heavily outside on the Robscott Manor development in Newark where Tamira was raised when she pulled up. She parked her car in Mr. Marvin and Mom Gina's driveway and just sat there staring in between their house and her old house next door. It was good to see that the new owners took pride in the house like her parents did because the house looked beautiful decorated the way it was. The new owners had it looking like a winter wonderland the way Rudolph led the nine other reindeer over the front lawn that had been changed into the North Pole, and for a brief second, Tamira smiled a smile that was no sooner there than it was when she thought about what she had just done. Then the tears that stained her cheeks began to fall again.

Tamira was confused. She could not get her mind off of what had just happened to her life in just a few seconds. How just a few weeks ago her life was like a dream, and now that dream had went from sugar to shit, all because she decided to help Brooklyn and Boochie move. Had she just stayed her ass home, she would've never seen her teddy bear. The one she had seat belted in next to her, and she would've never found out that Greeny was behind her parents' death. But she had, and she did, and just being able to avenge her parents' death helped her close that chapter in her life. The chapter of having to live her life knowing that her parents' killers were still out there running free and justice would never be served. So just in that aspect alone, she was grateful; however the choice she made to avenge her parents' death could be the result of her losing her freedom. That's what worried her the most now. Not the fact that she had left a trail of bodies including her own son's, but the fact that there was a possibility that she would get caught. And even knowing that she wouldn't hesitate to do it all again if time would have permitted it.

"Fuck it!" she said to herself, then spoke aloud, "at least I got 'em daddy," she said and smiled knowing her father would be proud of her. With that, she got up the nerve to get out of her car and walk up to Mr. Marvin and Mom Gina's door, despite knowing Kiesha was inside. They hadn't spoke since that day outside of Padua High School when Tamira saw her in the car with Jay Bird, and she really needed to see her now. She missed her sister and knew that Kiesha would be the only one in the world she could share what she just done with.

Tamira knocked on the door and stood there with her head down, tears falling from her eyes, as she waited for someone to get the door. She was in desperate need of some love and comfort and knew that this was the only place she could genuinely get it from; family, not her biological family but her real family. The ones who genuinely loved her without a motive or ulterior motive for any gain of any kind. Just then the door opened up and there stood Mom Gina.

"Merry Christmas Tamira baby!" Mom Gina replied and opened up her arms for Tamira to walk into them, in which Tamira did. "What's wrong?"

"I just wanted to come home," Tamira told her as she found solitude in the breasts of Mom Gina, the same breasts that comforted her back to health when her parents died right in front of her. "This is home right?"

"Baby this will always be your home. As long as me and your daddy are still living," Mom Gina replied, and just by referring to themselves as Tamira's mother and father, Mom Gina had solidified their positions to her in her life. They were still mom and dad. "Now come on in here and get out of this snow. Marvin!" she called out. "Look what Santa Claus just blew in," and Marvin smiled from ear to ear.

"Hey baby! Merry Christmas. Where's that little man of a grandson of mines at?" he asked referring to her son.

"Home with his daddy. I haven't been there yet. Actually I'm just now leaving the mall doing some last minute shopping," she said stabilizing her alibi.

"Oh well you make sure you bring him over here tomorrow so he can open his gifts ok?" Mr. Marvin said then hollered up the stairs to Kiesha. "Kiesha com downstairs for a minute someone is here to see you."

"Alright here I come!" she yelled downstairs from her room over top of the loud sounds of Lil Wayne & Drake singing: "I wish I could fuck every girl in the world". Just hearing her sister's voice had put butterflies in Tamira's stomach because they hadn't spoken to one another in three years, and she wondered how Kiesha would act. Shit a lot has changed in their lives in three years. Kiesha had gone off to college at FAMU (Florida A & M University) and was a year away from a degree, and Tamira had been through a life not suitable for anyone. She had experienced the life Mom Gina and Mr. Marvin fought so hard in court for her not to have and now she was a killer. Not because of coincidence, but because of purpose. Tamira had become a killer a long time ago; the day she witnessed her mother being raped and killed and her father being shot down. When she saw how cruel the world could be for people so good like her parents, she knew then that it was a dog eat dog world and from that day on something inside of Tamira happened. Blood no longer pumped through her veins. Her heart now pumped ice water. She was as cold as Steve, stone cold Steve and wouldn't hesitate to kill again.

Kiesha had turned down the radio and wondered who was there to see her. "Probably Jay Bird," she thought thinking about her first because no one else came to mind. She had already seen most of her old friends from Padua because like her too, they were home from school for their holiday break. Then Tamira came to mind. Tamira Stevens, her sister from another mother and boy how she missed her. Tamira was like her twin, the only person who knew her, the real her. And she was excited at just the thought of seeing her and being able to share with her what was going on in her life. Then reality had sunk in, she hadn't seen or talked to Tamira in three years. Her mother had sent her some pictures of her, the baby, and Greeny though. They hung on her bedroom mirror at the apartment she shared with her "Delta" sisters. "Sheeeeee Weeeee!" she thought of their call and smiled. Closing her door behind her, she headed for the steps. When she reached the bottom and saw who it was she broke out into an all out sprint. "Aggghhhh!" she screamed happily as she charged Tamira.

"Eeeeeellllll!" Tamira screamed back and the two of them collided so hard that they knocked each other on the floor with love.

"Oh my God! Look at you," Kiesha said. "Look how "phat" your ass got girl! I never thought your skinny butt would ever grow an ass let alone some titties," Kiesha teased. "Are they implants?"

"Fuck you bitch! Hell no they ain't implants. They come from having my son," Tamira said lost in the moment. For a second there she still thought she was a proud mother. Then for the first time since she done it, she felt the pain of losing her child. A child that she had carried in her womb for nine months and the tears started again.

"Mira what's wrong?" Kiesha asked.

"I'll tell you later," Tamira said and for the next couple of hours until she turned her cell phone back on she enjoyed the time she got to share with her family. Tamira got up with her glass of spiked eggnog, walked over to the window, and looked out over the neighborhood as the snow painted it white. "Damn," she thought, "it turned out to be a Merry Fuckin' Christmas."

■■■■■■

Brooklyn and Boochie decided that since they didn't have nothing else to do they'd head over to Tamira and Greeny's spot. They had just talked to her a little over an hour ago and she said she was cooking dinner, so why not grab a plate and drop their gifts off. "That's like killing two birds with one stone," they agreed and headed out. Boochie was behind the wheel and nearing Tamira's neighborhood when she noticed all these fucking fire trucks approaching her rearview mirror. "Damn! Look at all these fire trucks and ambulances coming," Boochie said to Brooklyn who turned around in her seat to see.

"Damn! Girl that is a lot, it must be a bad fire somewhere," Brooklyn said then out of the corner of her eye she notice what appeared to be Tamira's brake lights bending the corner leading out of the development. "Did you see that?" Brooklyn asked Boochie.

"See what baby? That car?" Boochie asked but didn't wait for a response. "Nah I thought it was her too."

"Oh?" she said then turned back around in her seat.

The closer they got to Tamira and Greeny's condo, the more concern crossed their minds because the fire trucks and shit was still heading in the same direction as them. And although they were sure they weren't headed to where their loved ones were, there was still that fear of: "What if?" so when Boochie turned onto their street and saw it lit up like the Fourth of July in front of Tamira and Greeny's building they became frantic with panic!

"Oh my God!" Brooklyn screamed and grabbed at the car door before it even stopped.

"What da fu," Boochie stopped in mid-sentence as an explosion erupted from Tamira and Greeny's window, and the car came to a sliding stop thanks to the freshly fallen snow that covered the road. "Brooklyn hold up!" Boochie called out to her girlfriend, but she was already at top speed and running towards the fire.

"Ma'am get back!!" one of the fire fighters yelled to her, but she disregarded his command and kept right on towards the burning building. "Ma'am stop!" he yelled again but this time another fire fighter grabbed her and held her around the waist as her arms flailed and she leaned forward in his arms screaming, "My brother, sister, and their baby is in there!!" she cried. "Please save my brother and sister!!"

"Ma'am we're doing all we can," the chief who came to the aide of the fire fighter said, "But it's a bad one. We have men inside," he told her and jus then one came running out carrying what looked like a dead body, and Brooklyn went bananas!! It was her big brother Greeny, her hero, father, protector, her everything! It can't be him! But it was and they were throwing a sheet over his burned up body. Not even over the initial shock of that yet, she was hit with another tragedy. A fire fighter was carrying out her nephew and placing him under the sheet with his father. But where was Tamira's body at? They still hadn't pulled out her body yet? And Brooklyn was beginning to think as she looked around for Tamira's car. It wasn't there so it was a good possibility she was still alive. Almost hysterical she turned to Boochie and said, "call Tamira." The phone went straight to the answering machine. Hearing that, Brooklyn and Boochie both felt something wasn't right.

"Where she at?" Brooklyn asked Boochie like she knew.

"I don't know? She might've gone to the store," Boochie said, then tried to comfort Brooklyn, but the sight of the sheet, her brother, and her nephew was too much. Her cries could be heard blocks away.

"Excuse me ma'am," a police officer in plain clothes said as he approached them. "Do any of you know the people who lived at this address right here?"

"Yes," Boochie spoke for Brooklyn.

"Relative?"

"Yes it was my wife's brother," Boochie answered.

"I'm sorry. Well as of now we're treating this blaze as a crime scene. Do you know of anyone who might have wanted to harm Mr. Wright, uh Greeny?"

"No, and how do you know Hakeeme as Greeny?"

"Well ma'am Mr. Wright has had many run-ins with the law. He was known by the first name, nickname basis down at the station. That's why I asked you did you know of anyone who could've wanted harm done to him. Maybe the victims of the deceased family of the trial he just beat? Maybe one of his many robbery victims? Uh any other idea?" he asked in a sarcastic tone, one that caught Brooklyn's attention right away.

"You know what pig!? Get da fuck away from us with all dat bullshit hear? My brother just died in a fire and you're talkin' about him like a dog or some shit! Yeah he may have had a few run-ins with the law, but he was still my brother. Now if you would excuse us," Brooklyn said and Boochie led her away.

"Suit yourself. One less problem we have to worry about," the detective said. "I'll just label it a cold case and move on to something else. Nobody cares about a drug dealing, stick-up kid whose been accused of murder. Shit, half the force will be glad to know that Mr. Wright a.k.a. Greeny was found with bullets to the head and chest," he told himself as he walked back to the crime scene. Then something hit the detective like a ton of bricks. Damn, first Kyle was left for dead and now totally blind and speechless because of the removal of this tongue. Then Snotty was found shot and killed down Route 9 and now this. Greeny being murdered and set to blaze. Shit like this didn't happen coincidentally. This shit was patterned. All three friends that were under investigation by the Wilmington, State, and County police officers were dead. Everything about it stunk. He was going to get to the bottom of it.

Other Novels

By

Leondrei Prince

Bloody Money
Me & My Girls
Bloody Money 2
Bloody Money III City Under Siege
The Tommy Good Story
The Tommy Goods Story II
The Tommy Goods Story III
Merry F##kin' Xmas

...Coming Soon...

The Rise & Fall of The Capelli Family
And
Frankie 'Lil' Frankie' Maraachi, III

Happy F##kin' New Year!

Street Knowledge Publishing LLC
P.O. Box 345
Wilmington, DE 19899
TOLL FREE:1.888.401.1114
www.skbookstore.com

Date: _____

Purchaser _____

Mailing Address _____

City_____ State_____ Zip Code_____

Qty.	Title of Book		Price Each	Total
	978-0-9822515-6-0	Bloody Money	$15.00	
	978-0-9822515-9-1	Bloody Money 2	$15.00	
	978-0-9799556-4-8	Bloody Money 3	$15.00	
	978-0-9799556-0-0	Tommy Good Story	$15.00	
	978-0-9822515-0-8	Tommy Good Story II	$15.00	
	978-0-9746199-1-0	Me & My Girls	$15.00	
	978-0-9746199-0-3	Cash Ave	$15.00	
	978-0-9822515-1-5	Merry F$$kin' Xmas	$15.00	
	978-0-9799556-1-7	A Day After Forever	$15.00	
	978-0-9822515-3-9	A Day After Forever 2	$15.00	
	978-0-9799556-2-4	Court & the Streets	$15.00	
	978-0-9822515-5-3	Court In The Street 2	$15.00	
	978-0-9746199-6-5	Don't Mix the Bitter with the Sweet	$15.00	
	978-0-9799556-9-3	Playing For Keeps	$15.00	
	978-0-9799556-3-1	Pain Freak	$15.00	
	978-0-9799556-5-5	Dipped Up	$15.00	
	978-0-9799556-6-2	No Love No Pain	$15.00	
	978-0-9746199-4-1	Dopesick	$15.00	
	978-0-9799556-7-9	Lust, Love & Lies	$15.00	
	978-0-9799556-8-6	Money and Murder	$15.00	
	978-0-9746199-7-2	The Queen Of New York	$15.00	
	978-0-9799556-5-5	Dipped Up	$15.00	
	978-0-9746199-8-9	Sin 4 Life	$15.00	
	978-0-9822515-4-6	A Little More Sin	$15.00	
	978-0-9746199-5-8	The Hunger	$15.00	
	978-09746199-3-4	Money Grip	$15.00	
	978-0-9822515-7-7	Young Rich & Dangerous	$15.00	
		Total Books Ordered	Quantity	
			Subtotal	
SHIPPING/HANDLING (Via U.S. Priority Mail) $5.25 for 1st book, $2.00 for each additional book			Shipping Total	
Institutional Check & Money Order (No Personal Check Accepted)		**Total** $		

194

Made in the USA
Middletown, DE
16 July 2024

57368596R00116